Ingunn Thon

A postcard to
OLLIS

Illustrated by
Nora Brech

Translated from Norwegian by
Siân Mackie

WACKY BEE

Published by

Wacky Bee Books

Shakespear House, 168 Lavender Hill, London, SW11 5TG, UK

ISBN: 978-1-9999033-4-3

First published in the UK 2019

© Ingunn Thon & Samlaget, Oslo 2018.
Published by agreement with Oslo Literary Agency.

Illustrations by Nora Brech © 2018

English translation Siân Mackie © 2019

This translation has been published with the financial support of NORLA

Design by David Rose

Printed by AkcentMEDIA

www.wackybeebooks.com

1

Ollis leans over the bathroom sink, her eyes closed and her teeth bared so they're easier to brush. She cracks one eye open and looks at herself in the mirror. Her pale face, the gap between her front teeth, and her bushy pink hair. It's usually blonde – the pink colour is just the result of an experiment that hadn't gone quite to plan. Let's put it this way: no one's managed to make a shampoo that keeps your hair clean for over a month, but at least Ollis can say she's tried.

Ollis is ten years old. She can't sleep with her bedroom door closed or jump from a moving swing. But she can make a mechanical whisk – one of those with two beaters, a crank and gearwheels – into a mechanical toothbrush. And she has. She's replaced the beaters with toothbrushes. She has to use the crank to make it go, but when she does, the brushes rotate like propellers and brush her teeth until they gleam. Front and back. Even the school dentist is impressed.

Ollis spits into the sink and puts her mechanical toothbrush away before making her way out into the hall. She walks past the door to her mum's room, with its little blue ceramic sign saying 'Elisabeth', past the door to her little brother's room, with its three pale grey pillowy letters spelling out I-A-N, and then past the door to her own room. Ollis's name is so long it carries on across the doorframe and the wall. It's made of lots of different coloured paperclips. Oda Lise Louise Ingrid Sonja Haalsen, it says. But hardly anyone knows that's her real name. Everyone in the village just calls her Ollis.

Ollis starts down the stairs before realising her mum is on her way up. She picked Ollis's long name. She named Ollis after five women who played important roles in Norwegian history. Her mum likes that sort of thing.

And here she is, bounding up the stairs with Ian in her arms and her red dressing gown flapping in the breeze.

"Morning!" she manages, a split second before she trips over her loose clothing.

"Eeek!" she shrieks, grabbing hold of the banister.

Ollis raises her eyebrows.

"Oh, don't look at me like that," her mum says, handing Ian over before tightening the belt of her dressing gown. "I'm not superwoman."

Ian is only five months old. In a way, that means he's not really a somebody yet.

He's more of a some*thing*. A thing that eats, cries and farts. Still, Ollis likes him. She hopes he'll grow up to be very inventive. Not more inventive than Ollis, obviously, but inventive enough. That way they can be an inventor dream team and call themselves 'Haalsen & Haalsen', and maybe win prizes in Germany and China, or other countries where you can win prizes. But that won't happen for a while yet. Right now he's just a thing that eats, cries and farts.

"I'll change him," Ollis says, starting to turn around again.

"No, no," her mum says, taking him back.

"You've really gone above and beyond recently." She ruffles Ollis's hair, making it even bushier. "Go eat your breakfast," she says, trotting up the last couple of stairs.

Ollis peers down into the hall. She can hear the clinking of cups and glasses, and the faint sound of someone humming.

Einar is Ian's dad. He moved in just after New Year. Ollis doesn't know much about him. She just knows he blushes a lot, is allergic to everything and likes everything to be tidy all the time. And he's always lifting Ian up into the air and asking, "Who's your daddy?"

This makes Ollis cringe so much that she has to leave the room. Einar says Ollis can call him Dad too, if she likes. But Ollis has her own dad. His name is Borge. Ollis calls him Borgepa, but he's never lived with Ollis and her mum.

Okay, Ollis thinks, *remember the countdown rule. If I hear Ian laugh before I've counted to five, I don't have to go into the kitchen. One. Two. Three.* Ollis cranes her neck and listens intently, but all she can hear is running water and her mum, babbling at Ian. *Four. Four and a half.* Ollis looks back over her shoulder. *Five.* No laughter. She sighs and stomps the rest of the way down the stairs, along the hall and through the door into the kitchen.

"Well, hello there, Ollis! You were in the bathroom so long we wondered whether you'd flushed yourself down the toilet!"

Einar is standing at the kitchen table brandishing a basket of morning rolls. She's tempted to turn right back round again, but she needs to eat something, so she just sighs and sits down. Einar smiles. It's a bit manic – his face looks like it's about to crack. His glasses are flecked with grease, as usual, and he smells like a strange mixture of bug spray and coffee. Not like nice, freshly ground coffee, but like cups that have been standing on the side all day. Einar pulls a face he probably thinks is funny and offers her the basket of rolls with such enthusiasm that she has to lean back to avoid being hit in the face.

"No roll to fill the hole?"

Ollis shakes her head, reaching for a slice of bread instead.

"Oh well, more for me," he says, laughing his stupid laugh. It's a sort of high-pitched, girly clucking noise. Ollis glances sideways at the kitchen door, wondering when her mum will be down.

"What's on the agenda for today, then? Exciting weekend planned?" Einar asks. Ollis shrugs and reaches for the cheese, cutting a few slices as quickly as she can.

"You're a lady of leisure today!" Einar taps out a little drum salute on the table. Ollis hates it when he

refers to her as a lady. She's ten. A girl. She wants to
roll her eyes, glare at him, whatever it takes to get him
to shut up. She wishes she was brave enough to pick
up her breakfast and leave, but she stays where she is.
At long last, she hears the bathroom door open. Her
mum clatters down the stairs, as she always does, along
the hall and into the kitchen with Ian in her arms.
She walks around the table and gives Einar a kiss. He
laughs his stupid clucking laugh again.

"Who's your daddy?" he asks Ian, grinning like an idiot. Fog fills Ollis's chest. Thick, thick fog seeping into every available space between her stomach and throat, pressing down on her lungs and making it difficult to breathe.

"I'm off out," Ollis says, escaping into the hall and shoving some bread and cheese into her pockets as she goes.

"See you later," her mum chirps.

Ollis pulls on her wellies before grabbing her red anorak and grey bag from the shoe rack in the hall. Then she pauses for a moment, looking more closely at the bag. It has 'Meinig Borge' written just inside it. It probably belonged to Borgepa when he was in the military. Ollis runs her thumb over the name before closing the bag and heading out.

2

Ollis puts on her anorak and swings the bag onto her shoulders. She takes a deep breath, drawing as much cool spring air into her lungs as she can. It helps. The fog in her chest lifts. Out in the yard, Micro the pug and Macro the St. Bernard are both snoozing in the doorways of their respective doghouses. Ollis walks over and scratches them behind their ears. Macro gives her arm a sloppy lick by way of thanks. She carries on across the yard and down the hill until she reaches the road. There, she climbs over the fence. She looks left, and then right. Then she looks left again, and right again. And left once more. Then she darts across the road, jogs over to a white picket fence and shouts up at the tall, narrow wooden house behind it.

"AHOY-HOY!"

The fourth-floor window crashes open, and there's Gro.

"AHOY-HOY!" she bellows back.

Gro Gran is eleven years old and in the year above Ollis at school. She can sleep with her door closed in a pitch dark room and jump from swings moving so fast they're in danger of going right over the top. Gro hates normal days and crying. She hasn't cried once in her entire life. Apart from when she was born, but everyone cries then. She has pale skin, blue eyes and the world's biggest grin. She mostly wears grey, green and brown. During the winter, she wears white. Camouflage.

"You never know when you might need to hide," she always says.

Then she goes on to say: "And you never know when you might need to pretend to be a boy." That's why her hair is so short. Gro Gran is always 'prepared'. She's been a girl scout for five years. That's half her life so far.

The two girls stand yelling "Ahoy-hoy!" at each other until it echoes in the mountains surrounding the village.

But no one bats an eyelid, because that's how the two best friends always say hello.

It started as a joke. One that made them laugh until their sides hurt. One that made them roll around on the floor holding their bellies with their mouths open so wide that Ollis could see the dangly bit behind Gro's tongue. That kind of joke. They don't remember what the joke was anymore, but that's still how they say hello.

"Wait there!" Gro shouts. Ollis hears her charge down the creaky old stairs, across the kitchen with its loose floorboards and through the door into the hall, the one with the shop bell over it. Then there she is.

"BYE!" Gro shouts over her shoulder, before slamming the door and turning to Ollis with her eyes crossed and her tongue hanging out. Ollis laughs.

"It's just a normal day," Gro says, grimacing.

"Is it?" Ollis asks.

Gro nods, spits in the flowerbed over the fence and drags a hand through her short hair. Some of the other kids at school call Gro 'bro'. They say she looks like a boy. But Gro just looks at them. Raises her eyebrows and glares. Stares them down until they shut up and slope off. Ollis doesn't like them calling Gro bro, but she does love seeing Gro in action. Gro's fearless. Ollis would give anything to be like Gro.

"I slept with the cable in last night," Gro says.

Ollis's eyes widen. She grabs Gro's face in her hands,

squishing her cheeks together until she looks like a fish. With a trout pout and big, round eyes.

"You slept with the cable in?" Ollis shrieks.

Gro has the craziest dreams, and one day it occurred to Ollis that it would be amazing to actually be able to record and watch them. That's why she had invented the dream recorder. They had found an old DVD recorder in Gro's attic and hooked it up to a cable, the idea being that before Gro went to sleep she would press record and put the other end of the cable in her mouth.

"How did it go? Have you watched it? Did it record anything? What did you see?" she chatters excitedly, her hands still clamped around Gro's face.

"Nuhn," Gro says.

"What?"

"Nuhn!"

"I have no idea what you're saying."

"NUHN…" Gro pushes Ollis's hands away and points emphatically at her cheeks.

"Oh, sorry," Ollis snorts. "But what did you get?"

"Nothing… I watched it for a while, but there's no picture or sound. Well, apart from white noise."

"Oh, bother," Ollis says, sighing disappointedly.

"Such is life, Ollis." Gro pats Ollis on the shoulder.

"But come on, time to find something to do before the normality of the day really starts getting to me." She wanders around the garden, looking for something to do. Then she stops and smiles.

"I almost forgot: Dad got the bikes out yesterday!"

There've always been two bikes at Gro's. One for Gro and one for Ollis. It's as if it was predetermined that Gro's best friend wouldn't have their o wn bike. They ran down to the shed behind Gro's house, and there they were. A green one and an orange one. Freshly washed and oiled, finally free from their winter prison. As usual, Gro takes the green one. Ollis takes the orange one. She puts on the helmet hanging from the handlebar and pulls the strap as tight as she can, shaking her head to make sure it's secure.

"I'm glad you wear a helmet, Ollis, but don't choke yourself," Gro says, laughing. She pushes her bike up to the road. Ollis blushes. She loosens the strap under her chin slightly and follows behind.

"So, where to?" Gro asks.

"The mountains?" Ollis suggests.

"There's nothing exciting about the mountains."

"Scrapheap?"

Ollis throws her right leg over the bike and puts her

foot on the pedal. Gro does the same.

"We go there all the time," Gro says. "What about up past yours?"

"Up past mine?" Ollis asks. "Where?"

Gro's eyes gleam.

"The birch forest," she says.

Ollis looks at the road winding its way up around the house. She pokes at the gravel with the toe of her welly. Being friends with Gro is brilliant, but sometimes it can also be a bit nerve-racking. Ollis isn't particularly keen on the birch forest. That, and her mum's said she's not allowed more than three kilometres from home. She's even given Ollis a pedometer. A gadget that counts all the metres Ollis walks. As long as she remembers to turn it on.

"Come on! It'll be fine," Gro says, smiling.

"Okay, but no further than three kilometres," Ollis says. Gro shakes her head, her smile getting even wider. Ollis digs the pedometer out of her bag, presses 'start' and attaches it to the handlebar. Then they're off, gravel flying up from under their wheels.

3

The further they go, the sweatier Ollis's hands seem to get. The road past Ollis's house and up the hill doesn't only lead to the birch forest – it also leads to Billy Kapra's farm. The farm where he keeps twenty white goats. They don't go up there very often because Billy Kapra owns the entire area and isn't keen on uninvited guests. He's chased Gro and Ollis several times. With his rake.

The last time they were there, Billy Kapra had spotted them while they were crossing his field and set the Goat of Christmas Past on them. The Goat of Christmas Past was so named because Billy Kapra had received him as a Christmas present from his mother one year. The goat was old and bad-tempered and long overdue for slaughter, but unfortunately he was still kicking. After a wild chase, Gro and Ollis had finally climbed a tree, Ollis so scared and out of breath by that point that she'd wondered whether she was having a heart attack. Yet here they are, paying a return visit. Flanked as Billy Kapra's land is by a steep mountainside on one side and a wide river on the other, they need to cross it to get to the forest.

Ollis wants to be calm and unaffected like Gro, but she can't stop her toes curling in her trainers as they cycle around the corner and up the hill, Billy Kapra's green barn coming into view.

"Stop!" Ollis brakes so hard that her bike tips forward onto its front wheel.

Gro jumps and veers off the road, where she and the bike crash to the ground.

The back wheel is still spinning when she picks herself up. She gives Ollis an alarmed look.

Ollis shrugs helplessly and gestures vaguely at her orange bike, red anorak and pink hair, which is sticking out from underneath her orange helmet.

"I'm a moving target. He'll be able to see me from ten kilometres away."

"What time's it?" Gro asks as if she hasn't heard a word of what Ollis is saying.

Ollis blinks in confusion, but checks her watch all the same.

"It's half elev-"

"Half eleven. Perfect! Billy'll be out with the herd."

Kapra might not like uninvited guests much, but he adores his goats. That's why he takes all twenty of them on a four-hour walk every day. Each of the goats has its own collar and lead, and they walk the same way through the mountains every single day.

Gro tells Ollis to leave her anorak, bike and helmet under a bush at the edge of the forest as she stomps between the trees and starts gathering sticks. She comes back with her arms full of pine branches.

"Camouflage has never been your strong suit," Gro says, starting to stuff foliage into Ollis's waistband. When she's finished, she takes a step back to admire her handiwork.

"Well, how do I look?"

"A bit like an upside-down Christmas tree," Gro says, smiling. Ollis frowns and peers down at the branches sticking out in every direction.

"That's a good thing!" Gro tells her. "We want you to look like a Christmas tree. That's the best we can do before Billy and the goats get back." She walks back up to the road. Ollis grabs the pedometer and puts it in her pocket before stumbling after her.

They crouch down behind Gro's bike, which has also been given the pine branch treatment, and jog towards the farm. They maintain their pace until they reach the corner of the green barn. Then they sneak along the wall to the next corner, the final stop before the farmyard. They won't be able to hide once they get out there.

"But," Gro reiterates, "it's half eleven, so they'll all be out on their walk." Gro cranes her neck, her entire head disappearing around the corner towards the farmhouse. She listens. She sniffs the air. Then she turns and smiles.

"Coast is clear."

They dart out from behind the barn and run across the farmyard towards the gravel track into the birch forest. Gro nods at Ollis, looking self-assured, but as they jog past the ramp up to the barn they hear a snort from around the side of the farmhouse. It's the Goat of Christmas Past. Ollis shrieks. He's bigger than she remembers and, if anything, looks even crazier than before. There's nowhere to hide. Ollis starts to panic. Gro, on the other hand, is cool as a cucumber.

"Look at the ground," she whispers.

Ollis frowns, confused.

"Behind the Goat," Gro hisses. There's a chain bolted to the wall of the house. The other end is attached to a leather collar around the Goat's neck, like he's some sort of guard dog. Ollis can't tell how long the chain is. What if the Goat can still reach them? She's about ready to turn back, but Gro starts moving again before she can say anything, pushing the bike in front of her like some sort of shield. Ollis doesn't want to stand there all alone, so she quickly follows, more or less plastering herself to Gro's back. The Goat snorts again, his ears twitching. They're only a few metres away from him now.

"Ba-a-a," Gro says, doing her best goat impression. This turns out not to have been the best idea. The Goat bleats angrily and throws himself towards them. Gro jumps on the bike.

"Save yourself!" she hollers.

Ollis throws herself in the general direction of the bike, only just managing to move her bum far enough to the left that she lands hard but precisely enough on the luggage rack. The Goat is heading straight for them.

"Help!" Ollis yelps.

But just as she's getting ready for the impact, the chain snaps taut and the Goat's bleating is cut short. Ollis turns to see the Goat staring at the chain in bewilderment. Gro whoops and laughs, standing up and pushing down on the pedals as hard as she can, propelling them towards the birch forest. It's all Ollis can do to hold on.

4

With Ollis on the luggage rack and Gro working the pedals, the bike winds its way along the meandering gravel track. It's the end of May. They've had sun and rain in more or less equal measure for the past couple of weeks, which means the birches have grown small, bright green buds. Rays of sunlight cut through the foliage, warming Ollis's face and extinguishing the last vestiges of her panic.

Ollis and Gro have been in the birch forest before, but much of it is still uncharted territory. It's huge. One time, they found an old tractor with a hare and her four babies in the shovel. There's also a small lake at the end of the gravel track that Ollis's mum says they shouldn't swim in because it's bottomless. Ollis isn't sure she believes her. If it's bottomless, that must mean the lake goes right down to the centre of the earth, or even through it, coming out on the other side, and if that were the case, it wouldn't be a lake, because the water would just fall through. Ollis and Gro have tried to find out exactly how deep it is. One time, they tied a stone to a spool of thread and threw it in. The spool spun and spun until all the thread was used up, but the stone still hadn't reached the bottom. It was kind of cool. Ollis smiles, thinking Gro might be right – this is a good place to spend a Saturday.

"Were you with your dad yesterday?" Gro asks suddenly.

"Einar's not my dad, Gro!" Ollis says, irritated, cuffing Gro on the back with her hand.

"Ouch! No, not Einar. Borgepa. I tried to call you but you didn't answer."

Ollis's pulse starts racing, her hands sweating.

Ollis has told Gro all about Borgepa. About how she sometimes visits him and they read old newspapers and cook sausages in the toaster and laugh themselves silly. And about how they go to cafés and write *Ollis and Borgepa are awesome!* under the tables in permanent marker.

"What did you get up to yesterday, then?" Gro stands up on the pedals again, and soon they're going so fast that Ollis has to hold on even tighter. Ollis knows that Gro is a bit jealous of Ollis and Borgepa.

She often moans about how boring and normal her parents are. Ollis doesn't really agree. She thinks they're nice. Sometimes Ollis is even a bit jealous of Gro and her parents. Besides, what Ollis has told Gro about Borgepa isn't entirely true. Not the thing about the newspapers, nor the thing about the toaster. In actual fact, none of it is true. She quickly changes the subject.

"Let's go to the lake!"

"Okay," Gro says.

Gro slows down as the gravel track ends, giving way to forest floor. They can see the glassy surface of the lake through the trees. Ollis clambers off the bike.

"Let's stash the bike," Ollis says. "In case Billy Kapra comes."

Gro smiles and rolls her eyes. They push the bike a short way past the lake and in towards a grove of trees. Gro moves some branches aside so they can lift the bike between the trunks. But then, as they bend to pick it up, Ollis sees something.

"What is *that*?" she asks, crouching down to look at something on the ground, her nose wrinkling. Gro follows her gaze.

There's a piece of rotten wood lying at the foot of the tree.

"There's something written on it," Gro says.

They set the bike aside and huddle together, squinting at the faded letters.

"Top?" Gro suggests.

"Top of what?" Ollis asks.

"Dunno, a hill?" Gro shrugs. Ollis nods and shrugs too.

Gro stands up again and has just started lifting the bike when Ollis suddenly realises what it says.

"Stop!"

Gro drops the bike, alarmed.

"What?! Is it a snake? Where?!"

But Ollis shakes her head.

"Stop! It says *stop*!"

There are a few words that can be used to stop Gro Gran, but unfortunately "Stop" isn't one of them. Ollis is well aware of this. She almost regrets adding the S when she sees how enthusiastically Gro's nostrils are quivering.

"A stop sign – with two exclamation marks! This couldn't be any better!"

Gro surveys the ground around them, starting to rummage around in the bushes and scrub, under trees and behind rocks. A few minutes later, she's found something.

"Look!" Gro pulls some grass aside.

"It looks like there used to be a path here." She turns to look at Ollis, her eyes bright.

Ollis turns and looks back the way they came. Is she brave enough to go home alone? That would leave Gro to play explorer to her heart's content. But Ollis doesn't want Gro to think she's scared. She decides to use her countdown rule. *If Gro says something before I've counted to five, I have to go with her,* Ollis thinks, starting to count as fast as she can. *One, two…*

"Come on!" Gro says, marching into the forest. Ollis sighs and follows her.

The path is indistinct. They can only just make out the trail through the undergrowth, but it's definitely there. They make their way deeper into the forest. After a few metres, Ollis is pleased to discover that the path is blocked by some bushes. She breathes a sigh of relief.

"Oh, no," she says, trying to sound disappointed. "That's a shame. The path ends here. Let's just-"

But before she has finished her sentence, Gro is down on all fours, squirming under the bushes. Her trousers and jacket get caught on twigs and brushwood, but she soon gets through to the other side. Somewhat reluctantly, Ollis tries to follow, but the branches Gro shoved in her waistband make it impossible. They poke her in the face, stopping her from getting down low enough. Ollis pulls them out and tries again. She refuses to be left behind. She makes herself as small as she can and wriggles underneath. Success! When she makes it to the other side, she finds Gro standing stock still, pointing straight ahead with a quivering finger.

"Look!" Gro says.

"Oh!" Ollis says.

Now her curiosity is piqued as well. There's another sign about forty metres ahead. They bound over to it.

The brown paint is old and flaking, the letters sloppy.

"Keep out!" Gro reads.

They just stand there for a moment, side by side, gazing at the rusty old signpost and wondering why it's there. It doesn't look like anyone has used the path for a hundred years. They've made a discovery. Found something no one knows about, or at least something everyone has forgotten about. A shiver runs through Ollis, from the top of her head to the tips of her toes. She can't chicken out now.

"What should we do?" Ollis asks.

"We find out why we're supposed to keep out," Gro says, turning to look at Ollis.

Ollis nods. They duck under the sign and straighten up again. They exchange a grave look. The deed is done. They've disobeyed. Ollis takes a deep breath and starts walking.

The path is so overgrown that they keep going the wrong way and having to find it again, running their hands over grass and scrub until they feel ruts left by wheels or depressions left by feet, or whatever else leaves tracks. Ollis fishes a packet of uncooked spaghetti out of her bag so that they can leave a trail behind them. That way they'll be able to find their way back. They walk deeper and deeper into the forest. Fifteen minutes pass. Then thirty. They're so deep in the forest they start to wonder whether they'll soon come out the other side. Ollis pulls her pedometer out of her pocket. 2.1 kilometres. She can only walk another 900 metres. She looks at Gro, marching ahead like she's on a mission, nose close to the ground and dry spaghetti clenched in her fists.

"Does nothing ever scare you?" Ollis asks.

Gro turns to look at Ollis.

"No. I don't see the point in being scared," she says, shrugging. "I think I've only been scared twice in my life. And I've only cried once, but that was…"

"… when you were born, I know," Ollis interrupts.

"That's right," Gro says, smiling proudly. "But everyone cries when they're born."

They keep walking.

Ollis wishes she was more like Gro. That being so far from home in a dark forest didn't scare her so much. But what if Billy Kapra put the sign up? What if he doesn't always walk in the mountains? Maybe the goats like the forest too. Ollis chews her lip nervously.

"What do you think they're trying to keep people away from? Something secret? Gro, what if it's something dangerous?" Ollis asks, trying to sound as nonchalant as possible.

"Dunno. Might be something secret and dangerous," Gro says absently. She turns to Ollis, who tries to look more excited than anxious.

"Or neither," Gro adds with a small smile.

"Maybe they just don't want people walking on the grass," Ollis says, partly as a joke and partly to calm herself down.

"Mm," Gro mumbles, scattering some spaghetti next to a rock.

"Maybe whatever they were trying to keep people away from isn't here anymore," Ollis says. "After all, the sign's pretty old."

Gro stops and looks at Ollis, frowning.

"Why would you say that?"

Yes, Gro is fearless, but tell her that something might turn out to be boring and she's terrified.

"I just… what if there's nothing to find?"

The furrows between Gro's eyebrows deepen.

"If there's nothing to find we could be walking for a long time. Until tomorrow, even. Or the day after, or the day after that. Or until we're all grown up! All without finding anything. Do you really think someone would hang up a *Keep out!* sign for no reason? Just to make us walk around a birch forest until we get old? Just so we-"

Gro stops mid-sentence, straightening up and squinting between the trees. Then she throws her hands in the air, flinging spaghetti everywhere. Fear grips Ollis as she turns around, terrified that Billy Kapra has caught up with them. But it's something else. There, just a few metres up ahead, is a large yellow letterbox.

5

Ollis and Gro run as fast as they can through the trees towards the letterbox. Ollis's heart is pounding in her chest, but not like when the Goat was chasing them. This is more like the time her mum brought Ian home from the hospital.

When they reach the letterbox, they stop and stare. It's mounted on a post. A crooked post.

"Should we look inside?" Gro asks, excited.

"No. You're not supposed to look at people's post."

"You're not supposed to *open* people's post. We'd just be looking in the letterbox," Gro says, giving Ollis puppy dog eyes.

Ollis looks around. Listens. She's fairly sure they're alone, but you can never be completely sure. Gro has her fists clenched so tightly her knuckles are white. Ollis can tell she's holding her breath. If she's going to be brave like Gro, this is her chance.

"Okay," Ollis says. "But don't touch anything."

Gro shakes her head excitedly. Ollis takes a deep breath, her pulse quickening as she lifts her hand towards the yellow flap, grips the edge and lifts it up. Both of them stand on their tiptoes, their chins resting on the edge of the letterbox, and peer inside.

"It's empty," Ollis says, exhaling.

"Ugh!" Gro moans, crossing her arms sulkily. "Why are they trying to keep us away if there's nothing in there?"

She's frowning so hard her eyebrows have knitted together across the bridge of her nose.

"They're probably just trying to stop people from looking at their post," Ollis says, closing the letterbox again. "I told you you're not supposed to look at other people's post. Mum says so."

"But that's just dumb!" Gro says, pouting. "In that case the sign should say KEEP OUT OF OUR POST."

Ollis doesn't say anything. She wants to be brave like Gro, but she's glad their adventure is ending here.

"So… should we head home?" Ollis asks.

Gro sighs. Then she lines up her right foot and lands a perfectly placed ninja kick on the yellow letterbox, right in the middle, making it tilt even further sideways. She turns and follows Ollis.

They've only taken a few steps when they hear a faint noise from the letterbox.

Whumph – thunk – clang.

Ollis grinds to a halt, foot still in the air, and looks at Gro. A split second later they're throwing the flap open again for another look.

"Post!" Gro yells.

Ollis just stares.

"But how…?" Gro starts.

"I don't know."

"But can we…?"

"I don't know."

"I mean, come on, it's…"

"I know."

Ollis squints at the postcard in the letterbox. It's propped up against one of the sides. Where did it come from? Was this a trap? Ollis looks around, but she can't see anyone. Her mum always says you're not supposed to look at other people's post, but there aren't any people or houses out here in the forest. Ollis twists her pink hair around her fingers as she thinks. Then, quick as a flash, she reaches into the letterbox and grabs the postcard. Gro gasps.

"We'll take it home with us," Ollis says quickly, putting it in her hoody pocket. "But I'm still not sure we should look at it. We'll need to find a very good reason."

Gro nods, her mouth still hanging open. They close the yellow letterbox and follow the trail of uncooked spaghetti back towards the bottomless lake. They're quiet all the way to the bushes. They're quiet as they crawl under the bushes, quiet as they lift the bike out from between the trees by the lake, and quiet as Gro starts pedalling home with Ollis on the luggage rack. Both of them are a bit distracted, trying to think of a good enough reason to look at other people's post.

But they still haven't thought of one by the time they reach Gro's house.

"What should we do with it?" Gro asks, eyeing Ollis's hoody pocket.

"Let's think about it until tomorrow."

Gro nods.

"Who's going to look after it?"

Ollis puts her hand in her pocket. When it comes to being patient, Ollis beats Gro every time. What Ollis can resist for five days, Gro can only resist for five seconds.

"I'll take it," Ollis says, leaning the orange bike against the fence.

"Okay, sounds good. Ahoy-hoy!" Gro chirps by way

of goodbye, waving at Ollis.

"Ahoy-hoy!" Ollis echoes, smiling, before turning to walk back up to her own house.

Ollis kicks off her shoes in the hall.

"Hi!" she calls, walking into the kitchen.

Her mum is at the kitchen table. Einar is sitting on her lap.

"Oh!" Einar says. He laughs his stupid clucking laugh and moves to the chair next to her.

"Hello, love," her mum says. "Where've you been?"

Ollis shoves her hand in her hoody pocket and fiddles with the postcard. Her mum wouldn't be sitting there with her arm around Einar for long if she were to find out where Ollis had been and what she and Gro had done.

"Nowhere," Ollis says, turning and heading upstairs.

They call goodnight, but she doesn't reply.

Ollis stops outside Ian's door. She opens it as quietly as she can and tiptoes in, avoiding the creaky floorboards as she makes her way over to the cot. Ian is lying on his back with his arms over his head. He's kicked his covers off. Ollis smiles. She crouches down so that her face is close to his.

"At least you're your usual self," she whispers.

Ian sighs in his sleep, kicking his little legs. Ollis pokes her index finger through the bars. He grabs hold of it in his sleep. Ollis gets a warm, fuzzy feeling in her chest. Einar might not be her father, but Ian is definitely her brother.

Ollis falls asleep the moment her head hits her pillow. She dreams about the postcard from the birch forest. In the dream, she writes messages to her mum on the postcard and tries to give it to her, but her mum doesn't have any arms, just a mouth that keeps saying "my little clever clogs" over and over again. Then, suddenly, her mum is as small as a baby, lying in the cot with Ian, both of them screaming "Da-da!" Then Einar comes in, but he doesn't really have a face – just a mouth with vile coffee breath. He reaches into his mouth and pulls out the yellow letterbox. It's tiny at first, but then it gets bigger and bigger and starts spewing postcards, hundreds of them flying everywhere. Ollis wants to shout for help, but she can't speak. She lies on the floor with her arms over her head as the postcards fly into her, making a frenzied tapping sound.

Tap-tap tap-tap-tap.

"HELP!" Ollis is awoken by her own shout.

It's dark and she's soaked in sweat. She throws her duvet off and sits up, gulping down air. She's definitely awake, but the tapping sound from the dream hasn't stopped.

Tap.

Ollis looks around.

Tap.

There it is again.

Tap tap.

It's coming from the window. Ollis gets up and looks out.

It's Gro. When she sees Ollis, she drops a handful of gravel on the ground and waves with both hands. Ollis waves back, opens the window and throws down the rope ladder. She hears Gro pulling herself up, and then her head appears over the window ledge. She tumbles inside, landing with a thud.

"Shhhh," Ollis says.

"Sorry…"

"What are you doing here? It's the middle of the night!"

"I've got it!" Gro is still on the floor. She squirms with excitement.

"Got what?"

"I've got a good reason to look at other people's post."

Ollis's eyes widen. She scurries over to her bedroom door and grabs a small red umbrella hanging from the back of it before tiptoeing back over to the bed and beckoning to Gro. Gro jumps into the bed and they pull the duvet over their heads. Ollis opens the umbrella and – hey presto! – it's suddenly light as day. She's attached an entire string of fairy lights to the inside of the umbrella.

"Wow!" Gro says.

Ollis smiles.

"I use it when Mum says I need to stop reading and sleep."

"Can I have it if you die?" Gro asks, eyes pleading.

Ollis laughs and nods.

"So what's this good reason you've come up with?"

Gro leans forward and grins.

"So you're not supposed to look at other people's post, right?"

Ollis shakes her head in agreement.

"But to know it's someone else's post, you need to find out who it's for!"

Gro's eyes gleam, and Ollis smiles. Gro has a point. Ollis shoves her hand in her pillowcase and pulls out the postcard. It has a picture of two giraffes on it. An adult and a baby. Gro is quivering with excitement, so

Ollis gives her the postcard.

"You look," Ollis says.

Gro is happy to oblige. She flips the postcard over and reads. Her forehead creases, smoothes out, then creases again. She stares at the postcard as if she can't believe her eyes. Ollis watches her impatiently.

"Well?"

Gro's forehead wrinkles even more. She gives Ollis a quizzical look.

"It's for you."

6

Ollis is speechless. A whole minute passes in silence as she sits there with the postcard in her hands. Staring at it with her mouth hanging open. It's starting to get hot under the umbrella and fairy lights. Gro squirms slightly.

"Ollis?"

"Hmm?" Ollis snaps out of her reverie so quickly that she makes Gro jump.

"It's for me."

Gro nods.

"It says happy birthday."

Gro nods again.

"But it's not my birthday. My birthday was months ago."

Ollis scrutinises the text, reading each and every word carefully.

Hi, Ollis. It's me. Happy birthday. I love you.

That's all it says. Whoever sent it has also drawn a sailing boat in the bottom right-hand corner. Ollis drags her thumb over the grooves left by the ballpoint pen. She can tell it's a boat even when she's not looking at it.

"Did it come from Africa? Do you know anyone in Africa?" Gro asks.

Ollis shakes her head.

"A mystery!" Gro whispers eagerly, clapping her hands as quietly as she can.

Ollis smiles weakly and nods.

"Okay. It's Sunday tomorrow. Let's get up early and go back to the yellow letterbox."

"Really?"

"Of course! There might be more postcards!" Gro gasps as if surprised by her own suggestion. "Ohhh, I can't wait! But we have to. Or… no, we do have to. I'm going home."

Gro burrows out from underneath the duvet like a mole, getting caught on the bedrail and tumbling to the floor.

"Why do you still have this?" she asks, slapping the bedrail. Ollis blushes and shrugs. Gro grabs the umbrella, closes it and pushes Ollis down onto her back before she can protest.

"Sleep! The sooner we go to bed and fall asleep, the sooner it'll be morning."

Ollis smiles, somewhat dazed, but does as Gro says and closes her eyes. Gro pads over to the window, where she turns and points at Ollis.

"Sleep!" Gro says emphatically before disappearing down the rope ladder.

Ollis opens her eyes as soon as she hears Gro's feet hit the gravel beneath the window. She fumbles around frantically until she finds the postcard and grabs the umbrella from the floor. Making sure no light can escape the confines of the duvet, she looks at it again. She looks at the two giraffes. Turns it over and looks at the writing. At the stamp and the postmark. The postmark is faint, but she's fairly sure it says June. That makes sense. That's when her birthday is. It's impossible to make out what year it was sent. It might be really old. Ollis pushes her duvet aside and walks over to the small iron safe on her desk. She keys in 2-9-0-6. The door opens with a faint click. Ollis takes out the only thing inside – a photograph. It says *Ollis and me* on the back and shows a baby sleeping in the arms of a man with dark hair and a beard. He's smiling, the skin around his eyes all crinkly, and there's a gap between his front teeth. Ollis touches her index finger to the gap between her own front teeth.

She puts the picture back in the safe along with the postcard and closes it.

Hi, Ollis.
It's me.
Happy birthday.
I love you.

7

Ollis and Gro visit the yellow letterbox in the birch forest two weekends in a row. Luckily, Billy Kapra always follows the same schedule. He leaves for his daily walk with his goats at eleven o'clock on the dot and comes back at half past two. That's why Ollis and Gro sneak into the forest on their bikes at five past eleven and sneak back out again at twenty-five past two. It doesn't give them long to investigate the letterbox. This would be a problem if there was actually anything to investigate, but annoyingly, the letterbox is always empty. No postcards, no letters… not even those circulars Ollis's mum finds so irritating.

Ollis sits close to the letterbox, waiting. Gro stomps around, griping about how boring this is all turning out to be.

"Ughhhh," Gro says.

Ollis gets up and opens the letterbox again, but it's still empty.

"Do you think the postcard was there the whole time?" Ollis asks, the sound of her voice bouncing off the back of the letterbox. Gro kicks a tuft of grass and shrugs.

"Maybe we just didn't see it at first and that's why it seemed like it appeared out of thin air."

Ollis looks up at Gro.

"But what if it *did* appear out of thin air?"

"I've said it before and I'll say it again: it's a bit difficult for me to answer that as long as it stays empty," Gro says, waving her arms in exasperation.

"But we're so close – I can feel it!" Ollis whines.

"Close?! We've been here a hundred times and the letterbox has been empty as a bird's nest in winter every time!"

Ollis raises her eyebrows.

"We haven't been here a hundred times, Gro. And I did actually hear something a little while ago. A sort of faint whooshing sound coming from…"

"A whooshing sound? That was *me*! I was so bored I was practising my whistling. *Me. Practising.* You know how much I hate practising, but sometimes even that's better than waiting yourself to death, and that's what'll happen if I have to make one more trip to this stupid letterbox."

"Fine," Ollis mumbles. "Let's call it a day."

It's four o'clock on a Saturday in June. They're on their way home from the letterbox for the fourth time. They can wear trainers now instead of wellies. The birch trees are in full leaf.

As soon as they're off Billy Kapra's land, Gro clears her throat.

"I'm not coming tomorrow."

Ollis gapes at Gro.

"What? But we haven't found anything out yet!"

"Exactly!"

Ollis gives Gro an incredulous look, but Gro's face is set. She knows full well that Ollis isn't brave enough to cross Billy Kapra's yard on her own, especially if she might run into the Goat of Christmas Past. She definitely won't try it without a bike.

"There's no point in you going back either, Ollis. There's nothing there," Gro says, pushing harder on the pedals to catch up. Ollis just leans forward over the handlebar and cycles even faster.

"We'll do something else tomorrow. We could prank call the mayor."

Ollis doesn't answer. Gro doesn't know what she's talking about. What if another postcard comes for her and she's not there to collect it?

Ollis leaves the bike outside Gro's gate. They say their ahoy-hoys and wave goodbye to each other. Ollis starts heading home, but then pauses and turns back.

"I'm going back into the forest tomorrow."

"But I told you I don't want to!" Gro groans.

"Then I'll go on my own."

Gro's jaw drops as Ollis turns away and starts walking again.

"Mum!" Ollis hollers as she comes through the door.

"In here!" says a voice from the living room.

Ollis goes in to find her mum and Einar giggling on the sofa with their arms around each other. *Eww,* Ollis thinks. Her mum turns to look at her, still grinning like a loon.

"Where've you been?"

"Nowhere," Ollis says.

"Oh, nowhere, was it?" her mum says, and Einar laughs the way grown-ups do when they think they've figured something out. If only they knew how little they understood. Ollis turns to leave.

"Hey, hold on, Ollis. What was it you wanted?" her mum asks, sounding a bit more like her usual self.

"It was nothing."

"Oh, come on. What's up?"

Ollis gives Einar a sideways glance and shakes her head.

"Oh, Ollis. You can tell Einar as well!"

Fog fills Ollis's chest again.

"Really, it was nothing."

"Ollis?" Einar tries.

Ollis turns and leaves. Einar can pretend he and Ollis are part of the same family as much as he wants, but they're not. Ollis goes upstairs and opens Ian's door.

"Hello?" she whispers.

"Oog!" Ian says.

Ollis walks over to the cot. Ian is lying on his back and grinning like he's won 1000 kroner on a scratch card. He's all gums and no teeth, drooling more than Macro.

"Ooba doo," Ian says.

"Libiddy beeboo," Ollis says, and Ian laughs himself silly. The fog lifts and she relaxes. She takes off her bag and digs around in it until she finds a small black tape recorder. She presses the record button.

"Bibba booby?" she asks Ian. His laughter warbles out of his strange little mouth.

Ollis does it again. Ian lets out a screech that turns into a happy gurgle. Ollis laughs too. Then, suddenly, she has an idea. She looks from the tape recorder to Ian and then back at the tape recorder. She shoves it in her bag before quickly smoothing a hand over Ian's head.

"Thank you!" she whispers.

Ollis bounds downstairs and out of the house. Sure, Gro might be the tough one, but she still needed Ollis to teach her that the only difference between a sheep and a lamb is age. Ollis knows things. True, she probably knows more about sheep than goats, but she's never heard anyone say that goats aren't scared of dogs.

"Macro! Come here, Macro!" she calls cheerily.

A second later their tiny pug, Micro, emerges and trots over to her. He scampers eagerly around her feet, his tongue hanging out and his eyes wide. Ollis crouches down and scratches him behind one tiny ear.

"Ah, sorry bud, you can't help me today."

Macro's tired eyes peer at her from the bigger of the two doghouses. Ollis takes out her tape recorder and presses record.

"Macro, look! Squirrel!" Ollis points at the forest.

Macro lifts his nose to the sky and gives five deep, booming barks. They're so loud that they make the tape recorder vibrate.

"Perfect!" Ollis murmurs, pressing stop. "If Gro won't help me across the farmyard, at least you will." The huge St. Bernard pants in response, reversing back into his doghouse and flopping down onto the ground.

8

A new day. It's half past eleven, and Ollis is keeping out of sight behind the barn. She's been there for half an hour. Billy Kapra has been gone for ages, but Ollis still hasn't worked up the courage to look out across the farmyard. She's wearing green, like Gro would. She's shoved some pine branches in her waistband as well. Gro would probably have done that too. Ollis doesn't have a bike, so she's walked all the way here from the house. She's sweating and the pine needles keep stabbing her neck. Stupid Gro. If she hadn't bailed on her, they'd have been at the letterbox ages ago. Ollis looks down at her tape recorder. It's slick with sweat from her clammy hands. What if it wasn't enough? She should have found a way to bring the bike. Ollis closes her eyes and exhales. *If I see a bird before I've counted to five, I can go home again. One.* Ollis looks up at the blue sky. *Two. Three.* She looks to the right, and then to the left. Nothing. *Four.* To the right again. *Five.* Nothing. Ollis takes a deep breath and throws herself around the corner, sprinting towards the birch forest. She hasn't run more than ten metres before the Goat of Christmas Past is blocking her path, his back arched like an angry cat. But Ollis is ready. She closes her eyes, presses play and holds the tape recorder up in front of her like a shield. Silence. Ollis looks at it and gives it a shake, and then, luckily, the recording starts. However, instead of a dog barking, all she can hear is the sound of a baby gurgling. Ian. The Goat snorts, his nostrils flaring. Ollis tries fast-forwarding, but Macro's barks aren't there. The Goat stamps his hoof and takes a step forward. Panicking, Ollis throws the tape recorder at him. That's when he snaps. The chain rattles as he charges at her. Ollis shrieks, covering her face with her hands and bolting back the way she came.

"WOOF! WOOF!" The sound echoes around the yard. Ollis whirls around to see the Goat scarpering around the corner of the farmhouse. *Was that the tape recorder?* she wonders, confused, but then a familiar voice pipes up behind her.

"What a performance!"

Ollis turns to see a grin as smug as it is broad. Gro

climbs off her bike and pushes it over from the corner of the barn.

"You were almost toast. But he wasn't expecting that, was he?" Gro says, winking. Ollis stares back at her, speechless.

"And neither were you," Gro says, smiling lopsidedly.

"What are you doing here?" Ollis asks.

"Well, I *am* the camouflage expert. The least I could do was make sure you were properly kitted out." Gro walks over to Ollis and plucks at the branches sticking out of her waistband. "But apparently I had no reason to worry." Gro laughs. "What was that you threw?"

Ollis picks the tape recorder up from the ground. She holds it out.

"I recorded Macro barking to scare the Goat."

"Genius!" Gro says, beaming. "It's always a shame when technology gets in the way of good ideas."

Ollis nods and puts the tape recorder back in her bag.

"I'll come with you to the letterbox. But this is the last time!" Gro says, looking away and fiddling with the bike's handlebar. Ollis throws her arms around her neck.

"Thank you, thank you, thank you!"

Gro snorts and pats the luggage rack.

"Jump on!"

Gro and Ollis cycle a bit more slowly than usual into the forest – they're not going to make it back before Billy Kapra, so why rush? Gro drags a hand through her hair, making it stick up all over the place.

"Dad was a bit annoyed yesterday," she says. "I think we damaged the luggage rack when we were trying to get away from the Goat."

"You didn't tell him where we'd been, did you?" Ollis asks uneasily.

"What, no! Are you mad? He's told me a thousand times not to set foot on Billy Kapra's land. I'd be washing the dishes for a month if he knew what we were doing." Ollis thinks about Borgepa. About how he's never made her wash the dishes. Her chest hurts.

They've made the trip to the letterbox so many times now that it's quick and easy. They know the best way of getting past the bushes by the lake, how low you need to duck to get under the *Keep out!* sign and how the path winds its way through the forest. They don't need to leave an uncooked spaghetti trail anymore. In fact, the path has become so easy to follow over the last few

days that they've started stepping in different places each time to make sure it doesn't become too clear. They don't want Billy Kapra to find out there's a secret path in his forest, or that it leads to a yellow letterbox. Not Billy Kapra, and not anyone else either. But as they round the final bend, picking their way around a big log, they realise it's a bit late for that. Because there, by the yellow letterbox, stands a tall, thin woman with curly grey hair, round glasses and an armful of post.

9

Gro and Ollis are so taken aback that they just stop and stare at the tall woman. Seconds tick by. More seconds than is really appropriate to stare at someone they don't know, even though seconds aren't that long. In the end, the woman breaks the silence with an abrupt and surprisingly guttural "ARGH!" before darting off into the forest.

"Oi!" Gro shouts, running after her.

Ollis isn't as keen to run deeper into an unfamiliar forest after a strange woman, but she doesn't want to be left behind, so she hurries after them.

The woman is fast, but Ollis can tell she's having trouble running while carrying so much post. She drops some letters, slows for a moment like she's going to pick them up, but then keeps running. Ollis grabs one, then another.

"OI!" Gro bellows again.

Ollis runs as fast as she can while also picking up the letters that the woman has dropped. She's so busy looking at the ground that she doesn't realise Gro has stopped. She runs into her and they both go flying, landing in the undergrowth. Ollis shakes her head, opens her eyes and finds herself looking at a small green house with black and white trim. Well camouflaged by dense birch trees. She also glimpses a curly grey head and a green woollen coat disappearing through the door before it slams shut.

"Argh!" Gro snarls.

Ollis isn't angry. She's so excited her heart is pounding against her ribs. She's managed to pick up five letters. She shuffles them, reading the names on the envelopes. The first one is for someone called Stein.

The second is for Ragnhild, the third for Kjersti, and the fourth for Ove. One last chance…

Please, please, please, Ollis thinks. She looks at the name. Eirik.

Ollis's heart, which had been on the verge of bursting out of her chest only a moment before, suddenly feels impossibly heavy. She takes off her bag and tucks the letters inside. That's when she finds her pedometer. Ollis gasps. She'd been so busy picking up letters that she'd completely forgotten to keep in mind how far she was running. She takes it out. 2.99 kilometres. Ollis breathes a sigh of relief. That was close. They need to go. But just as she's thinking this, Gro gets up, brushes grass and dirt from her trousers and starts marching determinedly towards the small house. She walks right up to the door.

"Psst," Ollis hisses, trying to stop her. Gro shakes her head. Ollis nods. Gro shakes her head again.

Ollis nods and jabs her finger at the pedometer in her hand. Gro stomps over to Ollis, grabs the pedometer and looks at it.

"I've come here with you a thousand times. The least you can do is walk ten steps further than your three-kilometre limit for me."

Ollis can't think of anything to say to that. Gro grips her arm and pulls her over to the house. She pushes down on the door handle and *click* – the door opens. Gro turns to Ollis wearing the world's biggest grin. Ollis flaps her arms ineffectually. They can't just wander into the house of a strange woman who clearly doesn't want anything to do with them, but Gro doesn't seem to care. Ollis sighs. Maybe Gro's right. Maybe Ollis owes her this, and anyway, if even one of the letters the woman has is for Ollis… She nods. Gro mimes clapping her hands excitedly before they huddle together and sneak into the hall.

It's dark inside, but Ollis can see a pair of boots and the green woollen coat the tall woman was just wearing. The house smells like pine trees. Gro creeps forwards into what looks like another hall, but with shelves piled high with books of all colours and sizes. There are even books on the floor. Loads of them! They discover this as Gro knocks over a tower of encyclopaedias. Ollis watches in horror as the books start to fall, and even though it seems to happen in slow motion, she's powerless to stop them. The books hit the floor with a crash. Ollis raises her arms over her head, expecting some sort of attack, but instead the books seem to have fulfilled some sort of doorbell function. A voice calls out to them from further inside the house.

"Welcome!"

Gro gives Ollis a pleading look, but she shakes her head. They need to get out of here before the woman tries to cook and eat them. "Hello? You can come in now!" the woman's deep voice calls again.

Not happening, Ollis thinks. They can't walk into some crazy woman's house just because she asks them to. It's the oldest trick in the book. Clearly Gro doesn't know this, because she squeals with delight and grabs Ollis's arm. Ollis tries to shake her off, visions of getting hacked to bits with a meat cleaver flashing in her mind, but Gro is too strong. She struggles feebly as she's pulled into the next room.

It's a kitchen. A yellow kitchen with a small table, well stocked wall cabinets and even more books. The tall woman is standing in the middle of it all. She's holding a floral-patterned coffee pot, not the meat cleaver Ollis had imagined.

"Well, then. I suppose I should apologise for running. I haven't had guests in over twenty years, you see," she says throatily. She reaches up into one of the cabinets and grabs a couple of coffee cups. "So now that I finally do have guests, it would be silly not to have freshly brewed coffee to offer!"

She pours coffee into the two cups and hands them to Gro and Ollis. Gro is so bewildered that she curtseys. Ollis has never seen her do anything like that before, so she does the same, just to be on the safe side. The tall woman with the grey curls and round glasses claps her hands together.

"Wonderful!"

10

The woman's name is Borgny Klokk. And she talks a
mile a minute.

"I'm a singer. And a poet. And a painter. And a
professor. Outdoor enthusiast, outdoor critic and
botanist. Self-appointed, right enough, but it's still very
impressive, if I do say so myself. I've lived here all my
life, all on my own. That's impressive too. Ha!"

Borgny sticks her nose in the air like a proud
rooster and leans back in her chair. Gro and Ollis
are sharing a chair on the opposite side of the table.
Borgny's reserved the third in case she feels like putting
her feet up.

"You live here all alone?" Gro asks, leaning even
further forward.

"Don't interrupt," Borgny snaps, giving Gro a stern
look before smiling warmly again. "Well, then. What
was your question?"

Gro looks at Ollis. Ollis shrugs.

"I was just wondering whether you really live here all alone."

"I do. I've lived alone my entire life. It's really quite impressive. No one else has managed it before," Borgny says.

"You can't have lived here alone your entire life," Gro says, crossing her arms.

"Hush, now! You speak so loudly I can't hear what you're saying!" Borgny shouts, her hands over her ears.

"Have you never been into the village?" Ollis asks.

"The village? Yes, of course, I go there sometimes to steal food and coffee."

Gro and Ollis gape at Borgny.

"Stealing's wrong!" Gro says.

"But I don't have any money!" Borgny exclaims, irritated. "And if I went during the day and tried to get a job, people would start to idolise me as soon as they shook my hand. They'd start inviting me for porridge and fruit compote, and I don't want fruit compote, I want peace and quiet!"

Borgny lifts her coffee cup and slams it down on the table three times, driving her point home.

"Peace and quiet!"

Ollis pinches Gro's thigh under the table, trying

to get her to change the subject. She doesn't want to know what happens when you annoy Borgny too much. Borgny grabs the floral-patterned coffee pot and fills her cup all the way to the brim in one precise movement so that it's close to overflowing. Then she puts her chin on the table, bringing her mouth to the cup to sip the coffee with a deafening slurp.

Gro cautiously clears her throat.

"Is that letterbox yours?" Ollis can tell Gro is trying to sound as pleasant as she can.

"I said don't interrupt!" Borgny says brusquely. She dumps a large spoonful of sugar into her cup and stirs like a woman possessed. Then she leans back again and looks out of the window. Ollis and Gro look at each other.

"Borgny?" Ollis tries.

"Bah!" Borgny jumps and spills her coffee on the table. "Oh, are you still here?" she asks, wiping up the coffee with the sleeve of her jumper.

"Er, we were just wondering whether that yellow letterbox is yours."

"Yes, it's mine."

"We found a postcard for Ollis in it," Gro says.

"Ollis? Who in the world is Ollis? I don't know any Ollis."

"I'm Ollis," Ollis says, raising her hand.

"Oh, you are, are you? I see. Well, it must have got lost then," Borgny says, as if it's the most obvious thing in the world.

"Got lost?" Ollis asks, trying not to say anything that might provoke Borgny. They really need to get some answers from her.

"Yes. Lost in the post. Had the wrong address on it or the wrong stamp or something like that."

"But then wouldn't it have been returned to the person who sent it?" Gro asks as nonchalantly as she can.

"Only if the person who sent it remembered to write their name and address on it. If they forget to do that, the letter doesn't have a clue where it's supposed to go."

Ollis looks at Gro, who looks just as confused as she is. Borgny sighs dramatically and leans across the table, gazing at Gro.

"Have you ever sent a letter and then found out later that the person it was for never got it?" Gro nods and Borgny turns to Ollis.

"Or have you ever waited for a letter you knew was coming, only for it to never show up? Haven't you ever wondered what happens to those letters? Well, they end up in my yellow letterbox. I don't know how, I don't know why. All I know is that the letters that come here are the ones that don't have anywhere to go."

Borgny drains the last few drops of coffee from her cup. Ollis and Gro are both so bewildered that they finished their coffee ages ago, even though neither of them really likes coffee.

"Wow!" Ollis and Gro say in chorus.

"Wow, indeed. That about sums it up. Every day I receive post for thousands of people I don't know at all, but not a single one of those letters or cards has ever been for me."

"So what do you do with it?" Ollis whispers, scared that Borgny might suddenly decide not to tell them more.

"Build bookcases, collect the post and sort it into folders on the shelves. Every single day," she says, throwing her hands in the air. Ollis scoots further forwards on the chair.

"So you collect post from the yellow letterbox every day?"

"It doesn't always come at the same time, but I always collect it at eleven o'clock. On the dot. Every day." Ollis and Gro look at each other, eyes wide. That explains why the letterbox is always empty when they get to it. Borgny blinks and squints at the ceiling. "Apart from today. Today I was a bit late because I got a bit wrapped up in my toffee spitting."

They look up at the ceiling, which is completely covered in blobs of toffee. Ollis thinks it's gross, but Gro looks impressed, much to Borgny's delight. But then Gro's eyes narrow. She turns and surveys the kitchen before getting up and sticking her head out into the hall.

"But if you collect the post every single day, there must be loads of it. Where is it? I haven't seen any sign of letters or wedding invitations…"

Borgny slams her hands down on the table so hard that her glasses end up askew.

"No sign of it, eh?"

She gets up so quickly that her chair falls over. Then she storms out of the kitchen. *Living alone your entire life is bound to make you a bit odd,* Ollis muses. She turns to look at Gro, but she looks equally perplexed.

"Come on, then!" Borgny yells from somewhere further inside the house.

Ollis and Gro get up and walk along the hall with all the books until they reach another door. Inside, they find a narrow bed with a crocheted quilt and a bedside table with a tiny nightlight. There's a trapdoor in the floor. It's open. They walk over, crouch down and peer down the stairs, their jaws dropping as they gape at the huge basement. There has to be a million folders down there. All of them are white, and all of them are neatly organised, side by side, on tall bookcases. There's no wall in sight. There are freestanding bookcases as well, at least twenty of them, arranged in rows with folders on both sides.

"How's this for a sign?" Borgny Klokk asks smugly.

"Wow!" Gro says, taking a few cautious steps down the narrow staircase. She jumps down to the bottom and spins slowly so she can take it all in. "Wow, wow, wow."

Ollis can't believe her eyes. She descends the fifteen steep steps and walks over to one of the rows of white folders, letting her finger trail along their spines. Some of them are thin, others really thick. Ollis tilts her head and sees that all of them have been labelled with names written in loopy handwriting. She squints at one of the thicker ones.

"Kaaarin Gr…ønneberg?" she whispers.

"Yes. I sort every single letter. Every name gets its own folder." Borgny reaches over Ollis's shoulder to grab a folder. It's big and heavy. Borgny has to use both hands to lift it, grimacing as she does so. Gro sees what she's doing and hurries over.

"Have you tried to get in touch with Karin Grønneberg then?" Ollis asks.

"No."

"What?! Why not?" she asks, alarmed. "It's not your post!"

"And I'm not a postman. The sorting's enough work as it is," Borgny says, looking up. She pulls several letters out of the folder, all of them with a slit in the envelope.

"You open them too?!" This is almost more than Gro can handle. "You're not supposed to look at other people's post! Right, Ollis?"

"Er, hello! I've lived here alone my entire life. The post's the only thing I have to look forward to every day," Borgny says, sounding petulant.

Ollis shakes her head at Gro. There's no point trying to instil manners in a woman who can use the fact she's lived alone her entire life as an excuse, even if that can't possibly be true. Gro starts walking up and down the rows.

"Is there a folder for Gro Gran?" She ends up on her tiptoes in front of Borgny, her face the picture of anticipation.

"No."

"Are you sure? There are a lot of folders here… you can't possibly remember-"

Borgny stiffens, her voice suddenly fierce.

"I'll have you know I know exactly what is and isn't on my shelves!"

"Fine, fine…" Gro raises her hands in surrender, trying to calm Borgny. Ollis tries to sound indifferent when she speaks up.

"What about Ollis Haalsen, then?"

As soon as she asks, her blood starts rushing in her ears. Borgny thinks for a couple of seconds before walking along one of the rows in the middle. Ollis's pulse starts racing. She doesn't dare watch. Instead, she closes her eyes and just listens to the sound of Borgny rummaging among the folders.

"Ollis Haalsen?" Borgny checks.

"Yes," Ollis says.

By this point Ollis's heart is trying to explode out of her chest. She can hardly breathe. She quickly crosses her fingers as well, just in case. She hears Borgny's footsteps coming closer, stopping right in front of her.

"Nope, no Ollis Haalsen."

It's evening by the time Ollis gets back home.

"Who's your daddy?" she hears from the kitchen as she opens the door.

"Ma!" Ian says. Her mum and Einar laugh. Ollis stands listening to them for a couple of seconds. She

grips the door handle and opens and closes the door
again with a crash. She waits. Then she waits a bit
more. But her mum doesn't come to investigate. Ollis
goes outside again and over to Micro's doghouse,
scooping him up and hiding him in her bag.

"Macro," she whispers. "Macrooo…" A pair of
sleepy eyes peer out at her.

"Come."

He tilts his head.

"That's right, come on, now."

Macro saunters out of his doghouse and follows
Ollis across the yard and through the door. She leads
him up the stairs as quietly as she can. She hangs her
'I'm sleeping!' sign from her door and closes it behind
her. Delighted to be inside, Micro jumps out of her bag
and up onto the bed. He starts scampering around on
it in such a frenzy that the duvet ends up on the floor.
Macro sniffs it, pleased, and settles down on top of
it. Ollis walks over to the small safe on her desk. She
keys in 2-9-0-6 and takes out the postcard and the old
photograph before carrying them over to her bed. She
sits down next to Micro, who wastes no time in licking
her face. Macro climbs up as well, making the bed
creak and groan under his weight. It's nice, listening
to the comforting sound of dogs panting and feeling

warm fur against her cold feet. Ollis looks at the back of the photo. A sailing boat has been drawn in the corner using a ballpoint pen. It's just like the one on the postcard. *It's me,* the postcard says.

But how is this possible?

After Gro spent a whole hour threatening to tell gossipy Nils at the corner shop that a woman living in the birch forest was stealing coffee from him, Borgny had said that they could visit her again on Saturday. They were going to help her collect and open the post – even though you're not really supposed to look at other people's post. Maybe her mum's rule doesn't apply to letters that end up in the yellow letterbox. Or maybe Ollis just doesn't care what her mum says anymore. After all, she's not really sure she can trust her anymore. Ollis hears a creak from the stairs. Footsteps coming closer and stopping outside her door.

"Ollis?" her mum says quietly. Ollis holds her breath.

"Ollis?" she tries once more. But Ollis lies still until she goes back downstairs.

She feels angry all of a sudden. Or is she upset? Either way, she's really confused. She has so many questions. Has her mum been lying to her? Did Borgepa die when Ollis was little? And if not, where is he?

11

Next morning, Ollis is woken by the front door
slamming. She opens her eyes and fumbles her way to
her watch on the bedside table. It's Monday, a school
day, and only ten minutes until she needs to get up.
She looks around. Her mum has been in to collect the
dogs. Suddenly wide awake, Ollis sits bolt upright. Her
mum's been in her room! She looks over at the safe.
It's open. Where are the postcard and the photo? She
fell asleep without putting them back. Ollis throws her
duvet aside. Nothing. Frantic, she shakes the duvet
over her head, but nothing falls out. Her pillow! She
pushes her hands underneath her pillow and her
fingers collide with something. She pulls out both the
photo and the postcard. Ollis heaves a sigh of relief
and puts them back in the safe. What would her mum
have done if she had found the postcard? Would she
have been as surprised as Ollis? Or would she have had

an explanation? Ollis asked her mum about Borgepa
a lot when she was little, but she always got the same
response. That Borgepa wasn't someone who *is*, but
someone who *was*. And that her mum thanked him
every day for giving her Ollis. Her mum has never
specifically said that he's dead, but she's never said he's
alive either. Ollis stopped asking about Borgepa a long
time ago.

Ollis can hear her mum singing in Ian's room.

"Give me your hand, my friend, as evening draws in
and darkness descends…"

She used to sing Ollis that song as well. Before.
When Ollis was little. When it was just the two of
them. Mum and Ollis. In the rowing boat on Lake
Nonsvatnet in the hot summer sun. Standing under
the eaves with her mum's big rainbow umbrella when
it was pouring with rain. Over their blue cocoa cups
every time the temperature dropped below minus
fifteen. On their knees in the dirt as soon as the
coltsfoot and dandelions bloomed. They always came
home with arms full of yellow flowers. So many that
they never had enough vases, which meant they had
to dig out all their jam jars and drinking glasses,
and sometimes even the eggcups. Ollis hasn't picked

coltsfoot or dandelions for years now. It feels weird doing it without her mum, and she's been too busy with Ian. And Einar. They'd never planned to have a child. They said it had been a happy accident. Einar moved in just before her mum gave birth. She said the least they could do was make a go of it, even though they hadn't been together that long. That it's important to be patient and kind. Ollis's chest tightens again. She's trying her best, but Einar just doesn't belong here. This is their house. Ian has to live here, of course, but surely Einar doesn't? At the very least he doesn't need to pretend the four of them are a family. Einar isn't Ollis's stepfather or half-father or whatever he's trying to be. Ollis looks over at the safe again. She wishes it wasn't Monday. If she didn't have school, she could cycle to Borgny's straight away and collect the post with her. Maybe something else would arrive from Borgepa today. Ollis groans and pulls on her trousers and T-shirt before trooping downstairs and into the kitchen.

Einar is in the kitchen. He turns when Ollis comes in.

"Why, hello there!" he says in a sing-song voice, waving his dish-soapy hands around so much that he ends up with splashes on his glasses.

"Dearie me," he giggles, taking them off and wiping them on the flowery apron he's wearing.

Ollis says nothing. Just walks over to the fridge and opens it. It's empty.

"Everything's here, Ollis. I'm giving the fridge a clean."

Ollis turns to see the cheese sweating on the counter.

"Elisabeth's not come down for breakfast yet. Ian was awake almost all night, so they need their rest," he says. "Take a seat. I'll make you something."

Ollis closes the fridge and walks over to the table. She sits down.

"The usual?" Einar asks, blinking.

Ollis shrugs.

"Righto," Einar says, starting to slice the bread.

Her mum used to make her breakfast for her every morning, but now it's always Einar. Ollis isn't sure when she last spent time alone with her mum.

"So it's two slices of the bread variety, with cheese of the cheddar variety?" Einar leans across the table.

He overextends like a monkey to hand her the plate instead of walking around the table like a normal person.

"Thanks," Ollis mumbles, only glancing up at him

as she takes the plate. Two new splashes of grease have already managed to fleck his glasses. Ollis takes a bite of her breakfast. The taste of greasy warm butter fills her mouth. Ollis retches.

"Hey, now! Enough of the amateur dramatics, hmm?" Einar admonishes her.

Ollis has told him a hundred times that she doesn't like butter. A hundred times! She gulps down her juice, hoping to get rid of the taste.

"Ollis?" Einar asks.

Ollis stares at the table, trying to resist the urge to throw her glass at him.

"Ollis?" he tries again.

Reluctantly, Ollis looks up. Einar chooses his words carefully.

"I know you know the dogs are supposed to sleep outside. You can't take them up to your room."

Ollis looks down at the table again. Her blood starts to boil. It was Einar who was in her room! He must have snuck in while she was asleep. Her pulse pounds in her head like a boxing glove. Ollis is so angry she wants to cry, but she won't. Not in front of Einar. She'll never cry in front of anyone ever again. Just like Gro.

"Hey," Einar says, his voice sharp. "Did you hear what I said?"

"Yes," Ollis says through clenched teeth.

"Good. Now stop being such a misery guts, okay? Oda Woe-da?"

"Oda Woe-da?!" Gro flops down onto the school steps next to Ollis.

Her eyebrows shoot up underneath her fringe.

"Yup. That's what he said," Ollis says. She picks up a stone and drags it along the step. It leaves a long, thin line.

"But you're Ollis, not Oda. In any case, did he seriously think that would take the edge off him having a go at you?"

Ollis smiles weakly and nods.

"Poor you," Gro says, shaking her head. "If I'd been there I'd have ninja-kicked him in the shin."

Ollis rests her chin on her knee, still doodling with the stone.

"Can I come to yours after school?" she asks.

"Sure!" Gro says, flapping her arms excitedly. "I think my mum and dad are home though, so we won't be able to eat in the living room." Gro sighs.

"That's fine," Ollis says.

She presses the stone hard against the step and draws a little sailing boat.

"Are we going to Borgny's on Saturday?"

"Of course," Gro says. "As early as possible."

The summer holidays start in a week. That means they might be able to spend more time at Borgny's. They might even be able to get there at the same time as the post. Ollis only needs one more postcard. She just needs to know whether Borgepa's alive. She so wants to tell Gro about the postcard. About how important it is and why, but she can't. Because then she'd have to admit she's been lying, and Gro hates liars. Ollis couldn't stand it if Gro hated her. She hadn't meant to lie about Borgepa. It had just happened. Ollis and Gro had hardly ever talked about him, but then suddenly, two years ago, the lie had just slipped out. Gro had been going on and on about a fishing trip she was taking with her dad. They were going to drive all the way to Finnmark to camp and fish for a whole week. Just the two of them. The words were out before Ollis knew what was happening. She'd said she was going to stay with Borgepa. That he only lived a couple of hours away. After that, Gro had started asking about him sometimes, and Ollis had just kept on lying. Ollis's stomach clenches. She looks over at Gro. The toughest girl in school. Proud owner of the biggest grin in the village. Her best friend in the whole wide world.

Dinner is already on the table when they get to Gro's. They smell it as soon as they walk through the door.

"NOOO!" Gro whines as she kicks off her shoes in the hall. "We're not having fish fingers, are we?!"

Ollis hears laughter from the kitchen.

"Bingo!" her dad calls through the door.

Gro stomps into the kitchen with Ollis on her heels. Her parents are already sitting at the table. Her mum waves a ketchup bottle at her disarmingly.

"Ugh," Gro says, sitting down and loading her plate with mashed potato.

Ollis sits down next to her. Gro takes a fish finger and puts it next to her mountain of potato before drowning the lot in ketchup.

"Just help yourself, Ollis. Don't be shy," Gro's dad says, smiling at her.

Ollis flushes despite herself. She nods, but before she can lift her plate, Gro grabs it.

"Let me! Do you like fish fingers?"

Ollis smiles and nods. Gro puts a bit of everything on Ollis's plate before handing it back.

"So, what did you do at school today?" Gro's dad asks.

"Oh, Dad, you'd have loved it! We learned about the digestive system," Gro tells them, sending potato flying everywhere as she starts gesticulating. Some of it lands in her mum's hair, but she just brushes it away and keeps listening as Gro gives them all the gory details. Einar would have scolded Ollis for making such a mess, but Gro's mum and dad chuckle and encourage her, talking just as much as she is. Ollis just sits and listens. She likes being here. The kitchen and bathroom are always a bit messy. Same goes for the living room. And someone's always laughing. Ollis looks up at Gro's mum and dad. They're hanging on every word Gro says. Like they're her biggest fans. They look at Gro just like Ollis's mum used to look at Ollis. Then, suddenly, Gro's mum turns to Ollis.

"How are you, Ollis?" she asks. "Do you like being a big sister?"

Ollis is so taken by surprise she almost chokes on a mouthful of fish finger. She nods and tries to swallow.

"It's Ian, right?" Gro's dad asks, smiling. Ollis nods again.

"How are you getting on with Einar? Is he nice?"

Ollis's throat suddenly feels tight. She tries to force the food down, but it won't go. She tries to speak, but she's scared she might cry. She tries to blink the tears away, but to no avail. She looks down and nods, hoping someone will change the subject.

"What, no! He's not nice!" Gro yells. "He called Ollis a misery guts!"

"Gro, calm down," Gro's mum says. "He probably didn't mean anything by it."

"Didn't mean anything by it?!" Gro's brow creases. "Then why say it?"

"He was probably just teasing. Trying to lighten the mood, or…"

"Well, that's just stupid!" Gro slams her fork down on the table and gives her mum a stern look.

"Hey!" her mum says, returning the stern look.

"Well, what if I started saying 'you're a poohead' instead of 'I love you', just to lighten the mood?"

No one says anything for a few seconds. Then Gro's mum smiles, just like Gro does when you tickle her. Then she starts laughing. She laughs and laughs until her eyes water.

"You're right, Gro," she finally chokes out. "It's really stupid."

Then she starts laughing again, which makes Gro's dad laugh, and then Gro, and then, finally, Ollis as well. They slump forward onto the table, two children and two grown-ups, red in the face, laughing so hard they can barely breathe. Ollis misses her mum more than ever.

It's late when Ollis gets home. The house is silent. She slips off her shoes in the hall and puts her bag down next to them.

"Mum?" she calls quietly.

She sticks her head round the living room door. It's dark. She opens the kitchen door. The light is on, but there's no one in there. She's about to leave when she spots a note on the kitchen table. She walks over and picks it up.

Hi, honey. Ollis's heart skips a beat. It's been so long since her mum's called her anything other than Ollis. She'd forgotten how good it felt.

I miss you so much when you're not around. Ollis can feel herself getting misty-eyed again, but this time they're happy tears.

Just wanted to say I love you. Kisses, Elisabeth.

All the air whooshes out of Ollis like she's just been punched in the gut. It's signed Elisabeth, not Mum. The note isn't for her. It's for Einar. Ollis wipes her tears away with the back of her hand, crumples the note into a ball and throws it in the bin.

12

Saturday morning. Finally. Ollis is out of bed before the birds have started singing.

She pulls on her trousers and jumper and thunders down the stairs. She'll take a banana or something with her, maybe two so Gro can have one as well. She opens the kitchen door.

"Hi." Her mum is sitting at the kitchen table. "Have you seen a note lying around?"

Ollis doesn't answer. She hovers in the doorway for a few seconds, not sure whether to venture in.

"Hmm, guess not," her mum says, raising her eyebrows inquisitively. "So… we never talked about where you got to on Monday evening. Want to talk about it?"

Ollis shrugs and walks over to the fruit bowl on the counter without making eye contact.

"Nowhere," she says, separating two bananas from

the bunch.

"I swear that's the only word you know recently. Come on, where were you?"

"At Gro's."

"Then why not tell me that? It's kind of important that I know where you are."

"Oh, sorry," Ollis says, heading back out into the hall.

"Where are you going now?" her mum asks, sighing.

"Nowhere," Ollis says, closing the kitchen door without looking back.

Ollis shoves the bananas into her bag, pausing for a moment to look at the five letters Borgny dropped last weekend. She'll probably want them back. Ollis closes her bag and shoulders it. Then she pauses again. *If Mum comes through the kitchen door before I've counted to five, she still loves me,* Ollis thinks. *One. Two. Three.* Ollis puts her hand on the latch. *Three and a half. Four.* She presses it down. *Five.* Ollis pulls the door open and steps through, slamming it behind her.

Borgny, Gro and Ollis stand at the top of the basement steps.

"Have there been any postcards or letters for Ollis Haalsen?" Ollis peers longingly down through the trapdoor.

"Or Gro Gran?" Gro asks, waving the letter opener and pen that Borgny has just given her around enthusiastically.

"Nope," Borgny says.

She moves to stand in front of them. Ramrod straight with her hands behind her back, like an army officer.

"Okay!" she says. "There are three hundred and twenty letters down in the basement that need opening and sorting. Once you've opened them, give them to me and I'll read them. Once I've read them, put them in the right folders. Understood?"

"Hold on, so you're not going to let *us* read them?" Ollis asks, gaping at her.

"Hah!" Borgny barks. "Of course not."

"But *you're* reading them!"

"I *need* to! It's my job. They're my letters. All of them. Absolutely all of them!"

"They're not your letters-" Gro protests.

"They're not your letters," Borgny parrots back at Gro in a high-pitched voice before sticking her tongue out at her. Ollis stares at Borgny, astonished. She's the strangest grown-up Ollis has ever met. Gro rolls her eyes. Borgny claps her hands together.

"Okay! Open the letters, give them to me, sort them into the folders. Come on, kiddiewinks!"

Ollis and Gro sit on the cold basement floor. Opening, sorting and filing, opening, sorting and filing. After a while, Borgny comes staggering down the basement steps carrying a small armchair upholstered in green velour. It's a bit big for carrying down a staircase, but Borgny stubbornly persists. She manages to whack both Ollis and Gro with it as she passes.

"Ouch!" Gro protests, glaring up at Borgny, but she pretends not to notice. She goes back upstairs to get herself some coffee and biscuits and then parks herself in the chair. She yells, "Done!" as loudly as she can every time she's finished with a letter, even though Gro and Ollis are sitting right next to her. Then Gro or Ollis takes the letter from her and puts it in the right folder. Ollis has filed sixty-one letters. So far, none of them have been for her, but there are still over two hundred to go. There's still hope.

Borgny clearly enjoys reading the letters. Sometimes she cries and says, "Oh, how beautiful!" Other times she cackles and leans so far back that she ends up hanging over the arm of the chair. Gro tries to peek at the letters at first, particularly the ones that make Borgny roar with laughter, but she soon gives up when Borgny keeps throwing biscuits at her head.

There are crumbs everywhere.

Gro's sighs and groans are almost imperceptible when they start, but three hours later they're much louder and more frequent. Ollis has opened a hundred and eighty letters. Gro has opened fifty-one. She picks up letter fifty-two, looks at Borgny and sighs so loudly that it sounds more like she has something stuck in her throat.

Borgny frowns at Gro over the top of a twenty-page letter.

"Shh."

Gro glares up at Borgny before taking the deepest breath she can and sighing even more emphatically.

"Shh, I said!" Borgny says, putting the letter aside and leaning down into Gro's personal space.

Gro gets up and crosses her arms, narrowing her eyes at Borgny.

"Peep."

Borgny leaps out of her chair and throws the letter into the air, paper flying everywhere.

"That's it! Out!"

Gro turns with her nose in the air and marches up the basement steps.

"Out, I said!"

Ollis looks up and realises Borgny is looking at her.

"Me too?" she asks nervously.

"Yes, all brats under the age of forty-two!"

"But… but I… it wasn't me…" Ollis stammers.

"Get out!" Borgny bellows, jabbing her finger at the trapdoor at the top of the steps.

Ollis gathers her things and puts them in her bag before scurrying up the steps. Gro is standing at the top, nose still in the air.

"Let's go!"

"But Gro, can't we-" Gro lifts a hand to silence Ollis.

"I'm never setting foot here again." She turns and marches out into the hall. Ollis watches her go for a couple of seconds before groaning and stomping after her. She follows her along the hall and out of the door, which she slams behind her. She can't remember ever having been this annoyed with Gro.

"Pah! Good riddance," Gro says when Ollis catches up with her. Ollis stares sullenly at the ground, swinging her bag onto her back. *My bag,* she thinks suddenly. *The letters in my bag.*

"You alright?"

"I… I forgot something," Ollis says. "Wait here."

Ollis is running back towards the house before Gro can protest. She bursts through Borgny's door without knocking, even though her mum says you should always knock. She runs along the hall and down the steps into the basement. Borgny is out of her chair in an instant.

"Hey, I said get out!" she yells, jabbing a finger up the stairs.

"No!" Ollis shouts, a bit surprised by her own daring. "Listen to me. I want to help you!"

"I said no-"

"Shh!" Ollis tells her. "I want to help you, and I have something you want."

"What?" Borgny asks, giving Ollis a deeply suspicious look.

"You said you read all the letters delivered to the yellow letterbox, right?"

"Yes."

"Last weekend, when we followed you, you dropped five letters." Borgny's eyes get even narrower.

"I have those letters," Ollis says.

"What? Give them to me! Now!" Borgny demands, reaching for Ollis. "They're mine!"

"No, they're not," Ollis says, slapping Borgny's hands away. Borgny pouts again.

"If they were yours, it would say Borgny Klokk on them."

"Well… but they… argh!" Borgny huffs.

"Here's my suggestion: every time I come here, you get one of the letters. In return, I get to go through all the post, and if there are any letters for Ollis Haalsen, I'm allowed to take them. Deal?"

Ollis holds her hand out.

"Will you have Little Miss Sass with you?"

"It'll just be me," Ollis says. "Okay?"

Borgny looks at Ollis, then at her hand. After a moment, she gives it a rough shake.

"Deal."

13

"Borgny's such a weirdo!" Gro scoffs.

Gro has been going on and on about how stupid Borgny is and how happy she is that she won't have to see her again all the way home. They've made it all the way back without Ollis saying much apart from "yes" or "hmm" here and there. She's really glad she managed to convince Borgny, but she feels bad at the same time. Really bad. Should she tell Gro she's going to go see Borgny on her own? Maybe she should just call it quits as well.

"All together now!" Gro says suddenly, thumping Ollis on the shoulder and starting to sing 'Borgny Klokk is a twit' to the tune of the birthday song.

"Borgny Klokk is a twit, Borgny Klokk is a twit, Borgny Klokk is a twiiiiiit, Borgny Klokk is a twit!" Ollis sings along unenthusiastically. Gro applauds herself, grinning broadly.

"Haha! Good riddance. Now we'll be able to do what we want when the summer holidays start!" Gro says, waving her arms around.

"Yeah," Ollis says.

They draw level with the driveway up to Gro's house.

"We need to get planning!"

"Yeah…" Ollis says again, hesitantly.

"What's up with you?" Gro asks.

"Nothing. Or… It's just… I might have done something stupid."

"What?" Gro asks, wrinkling her nose.

Ollis shoves her hands in her pockets and pokes at the gravel with the toe of her shoe.

"I'm… Well, I've asked… I've asked whether…"

"Just tell me," Gro says, crossing her arms.

"I'm going to visit Borgepa." Ollis regrets it as soon as she says it.

"Oh," Gro says. "For how long?"

"Just five days. From Saturday." Ollis pinches her thigh through her pocket. She hopes it leaves a bruise.

It's Thursday. Only two days until she goes to see Borgny on her own. It's so strange. Just a few weeks ago she'd have been appalled by the notion of going into the forest alone. But now that fear has been replaced by curiosity. It's like her brain shouts "POSTCARD!" as loudly as it can every time she gets scared. Her mum will be the easiest person to fool. Ollis will just say she's with Gro, like she always is. She's found another path to Billy Kapra's through the forest behind her house that she can use to get there without Gro finding out. She just needs to remember to camouflage herself. Her biggest problem is not having a bike. She'll need to get through the forest and back quickly to make sure she doesn't run into Billy Kapra. She needs a getaway vehicle. And something to scare away the Goat of Christmas Past. Ollis has tried to get some tips from Gro, but Gro never plans anything – she just does whatever comes to her in the moment. Ollis doesn't dare do the same. She needs to do it her own way.

Ollis darts across the yard to the garage. She opens the stiff old door as quietly as she can and sneaks inside. It's cold and dusty and smells like old potatoes. There's stuff everywhere, from wall to wall and floor to ceiling. Ollis starts rummaging. She finds a huge cardboard box, a shopping bag, some rope and twenty empty ink cartridges. She lifts an old tarpaulin and finds her old doll's pram. It has a red basket, a shiny metal frame and nice wide wheels. She gives it a good shake. It's very sturdy. Definitely something she can use. She's about to put it with everything else when she spots the turquoise oars hanging from the ceiling. Ollis recognises them straight away. They belong to the rowing boat down on Lake Nonsvatnet, the one Ollis and her mum use during the summer holidays every year. Ollis doubts they'll get round to it this year, especially since her mum has more or less forgotten she exists. But there, right next to the oars, is exactly what she needs: their rusty old kicksled. Ollis and her mum used to make good use of that too, Ollis sitting on the seat at the front while her mum stood on the runners behind, gripping the handlebar attached to the seatback and pushing off the snow-covered ground with one foot until they picked up speed. Ollis smiles at the memory and grabs the stepladder in the corner, positioning it underneath the kicksled and climbing up. Its runners are resting across a couple of beams. She lifts it slightly to check how heavy it is. Pretty heavy. Slowly but surely she pulls it out. It slides clear of the first beam without incident, but its weight becomes all too real as it loses contact with the second beam. Ollis tries to hold on, but can't, and the kicksled crashes to the floor. She freezes on top of the ladder. Outside, the grass swishes in the breeze. Footsteps come closer and closer. *No, no, no.* How is she going to explain trying to get the kicksled down in the middle of the summer? The door creaks and two pairs of eyes peer in at her. Canine eyes. Ollis breathes a sigh of relief. Micro toddles in, wagging his tiny tail. Ollis laughs.

"Go back and lie down." The dogs look at each other, then back at Ollis.

"Go and lie down," she repeats. They turn and shuffle out again.

Ollis looks at what she's collected in a pile on the floor. The doll's pram, kicksled, ink cartridges, rope and cardboard box. It's a better haul than she expected. She walks over to the toolbox sitting on one of the shelves. She finds a screwdriver, screws, a hammer and some nails. Next, she detaches the runners from the kicksled and the red basket from the pram frame. Then she attaches the kicksled to the pram frame. She screws it tight to make sure it's sturdy. Hey presto, pram sled. She cuts the rope into ten equal lengths, attaches an ink cartridge to the end of each piece and ties them to the back of the pram. That ought to keep the Goat of Christmas Past away. It might even help keep adders and badgers at bay. Ollis isn't a big fan of those either. She gathers up the remaining ink cartridges, puts them in the shopping bag and hangs them from the kicksled handlebar. Finally, she cuts away the top and bottom of the huge box and pulls it around the front of the pram sled so that one of the corners is pointing forwards, creating a makeshift goat plough. Let him try and stop her now. Ollis takes a couple of steps back to admire her handiwork. This might just work. She puts her creation in a corner and pulls the tarpaulin over it. Then, as she picks up the tools and goes to put them away, she realises someone is standing in the doorway. Ollis straightens up and takes a step back.

"Did I make you jump?" Einar asks.

"No. Or, well, a bit."

How long has he been standing there?

"What are you doing?" Einar asks. He's leaning across the doorway, making it difficult for Ollis to get past.

"Nothing," Ollis says. "Or… I was just looking for a screwdriver."

She takes a step towards him, hoping he'll move aside. He stays where he is.

"For one of your inventions?" He leans down into her space like she's a little kid.

"No," Ollis says. A bit too quickly. She blushes. "No. It's my bed… it's a bit wobbly."

"Oh, I can help you with that," Einar says, straightening up so that there's a gap between him and the doorframe.

"I can do it myself," Ollis tells him, quickly pushing past.

Einar watches her go, alarmed.

"Ollis, are you sure I can't help you?" he calls after her.

"I said no!" Ollis shouts over her shoulder. She's so annoyed that she wants to hit him. To knock him flat. First he sneaks up on her and blocks the exit, and then he gets annoyed when she pushes past? When she reaches the door, she turns to see that Einar is still sulking by the garage. Ollis hurries inside before he follows her.

14

The first day of the summer holidays is finally here.
Ollis has said goodbye to Gro on the pretence of going
to visit Borgepa. It's Saturday and her mum, Einar and
Ian are going fishing at the beach in Hamna. Ollis has
declined the invitation to join them. She's already told
her mum that she's going to be hanging out with Gro
all week. Ollis is pleased that they're not going to be
home, because that makes it easier for her to get the
pram sled out of the garage without being noticed.
Ollis puts on her wellies so the adders can't bite her.
She also fills them with dry twigs because she's heard
that badgers keep biting until something breaks. This
way, if they try to bite her, the twigs will break before
her leg. When she hears the sound of the car rolling
down the gravel track, she pulls on her green jumper,
puts one of the letters from the yellow letterbox in her
bag and runs out to the garage. She rolls the pram sled

out through the door, across the yard and up into the forest behind the house. There's no path as such – just a small opening between the trees. It's tough going, but Ollis needs to be at Billy Kapra's when he leaves. She picks up the pace.

Ollis comes out on the other side of the forest at two minutes past eleven. She watches, sweaty and out of breath, as Billy Kapra and his goats head off towards the mountains. Ollis looks to the right and then to the left. Then she grips the pram sled's handlebar, puts her foot on the frame and pushes off. She starts picking up speed straight away. It handles like a dream. She pushes against the ground again and swings onto the road up to the farm. Ollis smiles. It's steady too. As she approaches the farmyard, she speeds up and moves her right hand closer to the bag of ink cartridges. She spots the Goat of Christmas Past as she passes the barn. But Ollis is ready. The Goat stamps his hoof before charging towards her. With one quick flick of her wrist, Ollis turns the shopping bag inside out. The ink cartridges tumble out and hit the ground with a terrible clatter. The Goat rears up in fright and flees around the side of the farmhouse. Ollis rolls unimpeded into the birch forest with a big smile on her face.

When Ollis gets to Borgny's, the door is locked. Ollis knocks. Nothing happens. She knocks again. Still nothing. She takes a step back and peeks through the window. Two fearful eyes peer back at her from behind round glasses for a moment before Borgny ducks out of sight. Ollis hammers on the door.

"Borgny!"

"No, thank you!" says a voice from inside the house.

"Borgny, we shook on it!" Ollis yells.

"Yes, but then I changed my mind and had no way of telling you."

"You can't just go back on a promise!" Ollis is starting to get tired of Borgny's manners, or lack thereof.

"Yes, you can. That's what I'm doing now."

Ollis sighs. She shrugs off her bag and pulls out the letter.

"Okay, but that means you won't get this," Ollis says, waving the letter in the air. Silence.

She looks over at the window again. Borgny's face is pressed up against it, her glasses askew and her nose and lips smooshed flat. Ollis waves the letter again.

"Oh, alright," Borgny says, her voice muffled by the glass.

Ollis carries the day's post down into the basement. There are four hundred items to sort through. Borgny follows behind her, her coffee cup clattering against the saucer.

"Oh, by the way, I have news for you!" she says.

Ollis is so taken aback that she drops some of the letters down the last few steps.

"What? Really?" Her heart pounds in her chest.

"I've received…" Borgny grins and uses her free hand to simulate a drum roll on her thigh, "… no letters for you! Badum tish!" Borgny whoops, pretending to hit a cymbal. Gro's right. Borgny Klokk is a twit.

"Don't just stand there, then," Borgny says, stepping past Ollis and over the letters that have ended up on the floor.

"The day is never any fun until letter reading has begun. Ah, I truly am a poet," Borgny says, sitting back and stroking her chin. Ollis sits on the floor and starts opening envelopes.

The next two days pass in exactly the same way. Ollis arrives at Borgny's and Borgny says she doesn't want help. Then Ollis shows her one of the letters she's holding hostage and gets let in anyway. Then they sit down in the basement. Ollis on the floor and Borgny in her armchair. They don't talk much. Borgny only really speaks when she wants to scold Ollis. Sometimes for going too fast, sometimes for going too slowly, and sometimes because her writing isn't neat enough. Sometimes Borgny forgets Ollis is there and tells her off for sneaking into the house even though Ollis has been sitting there the whole time. Ollis has opened and sorted eight hundred and thirty letters in the last couple of days. None of them have been for her. By the time she's on her way home on the third day she's starting to get irritated. If Borgepa is alive, why has he only sent her one postcard? Did he just have a sudden urge one day, out of the blue, to send a birthday postcard to his daughter? Maybe the postcard is as old as the picture in her safe. Maybe he died right after he sent it. Ollis only has two more letters she can use as bargaining chips. Only two more chances to find out more about her dad.

When Ollis gets home, she goes straight upstairs. She closes her door, throws her bag on the floor and flops down onto her bed. She picks up her tablet from her bedside table and types in "finding your real father". Most of the hits are from people who don't know who their fathers are and who want to know how best to go about finding out. Almost all the responses say "ask your mother". Ollis tries typing "don't know who my father is" instead. But the responses are the same: "ask your mother". Typical grown-ups. Always telling you to ask a grown-up, because grown-ups know what to do, grown-ups can help you, grown-ups have all the answers. They really don't. Ollis's mum has lied to her and invited Einar to live in their house. She can't talk to her mum. Someone knocks on her door. Ollis stays silent. Did she remember to hang up the *Do not disturb* sign?

"Hello? Anyone home?" Einar opens the door. He pokes his head around the doorframe. He's wearing a bow tie fashioned from a napkin or a tissue or something. Ollis gives him a suspicious look. What does he want?

"I've brought you something." A cup appears beneath his head. A yellow one. The one only her mum uses.

"That's Mum's cup," Ollis says.

"Oh, is it? Oh well," Einar says. "I made you some tea."

He holds it out, the door opening even wider as the rest of him comes into view. He's playing dress-up.

He's wearing her mum's flowery apron, and there's a tea towel over his arm. That's when Ollis notices that he's slicked his hair back as well – posh waiter style. She doesn't know why, but it's *really* irritating. Einar takes a step into her room, the door opening all the way so Ollis can see that she did in fact remember to hang up the *Do not disturb* sign. *He wouldn't dare come all the way over here*, she thinks. Einar takes another couple of steps towards her. Ollis covertly closes the tab on her tablet. A second later, Einar cranes his neck to see what she's looking at.

"What are you doing?" he asks in a sing-song voice.

"Nothing," Ollis says.

Einar puts the cup of tea down on her bedside table. Ollis only likes blackberry tea, but this isn't the reddish purple colour – it's light brown. He reaches out and takes Ollis's tablet from her.

"Why don't you put this away for a while?" he asks. "You could come talk to us down in the kitchen."

Ollis's blood starts to boil. He has no right to take her things.

Einar gestures at the tea.

"I don't want it," Ollis says, turning to look at the wall.

"I made it for you," Einar says.

That's when Ollis snaps. Or – perhaps more

accurately – explodes.

"I still don't want it. You drink it," she snarls.

Silence falls. Einar just stands there. She turns and looks right at him.

"Go away! Are you blind? Didn't you see what the sign on the door says? Go away!" Einar gives Ollis a fearful look. He opens his mouth to say something, but then he grabs the tea towel from his arm, picks up the cup from the bedside table and leaves. Ollis lets out a breath she didn't know she was holding and revels in her victory. She didn't know she had it in her. If only Gro had been here. Then she'd know that Ollis is no coward.

The kitchen door opens and closes. Someone starts up the stairs. They're coming in fast.

Her mum knocks but doesn't wait for Ollis to answer.

"Ollis, what is going on?" she asks, bursting in with a concerned look on her face.

"What do you mean?" Ollis asks.

"Einar's trying to be nice to you and you're just being horrible!"

"No, I'm not."

"That's not what Einar says."

Her mum is on Einar's side. No surprises there. Fog

fills Ollis's chest again, seeping up into her throat to form a lump. She pinches her thigh. She won't cry.

"No, I… I just don't want tea."

"What is going on with you, Ollis? Why are you being so grumpy? I hardly recognise you anymore."

Ollis looks away. Plucks at her duvet.

"What's happened to my sweet little girl?"

The lump in Ollis's throat swells, now so big that it hurts. Ollis swallows and swallows. She wants to say it. To say she misses how it used to be. To say she misses her mum.

"Could you please start behaving like yourself again?" her mum asks, crossing her arms like she's angry with Ollis. Ollis blinks in disbelief. She doesn't get to be angry. She's the one who's ruined everything. Ollis is the one who gets to be angry. The fog grows thicker and darker than ever.

"Fine!" Ollis snaps. "I'll start behaving when you stop lying."

"What are you talking about?" her mum asks.

"Where's Borgepa?" The question cuts through the room.

Her mum sighs.

"Ollis, we've been over this so many times," she says, massaging her temples.

"Just answer the question," Ollis snaps, glaring at her.

"I've told you before, Ollis. Borgepa's-"

"*Someone who was.* Yes, so you keep saying. But that doesn't *mean* anything!"

"Ollis, there's no point talking about this now."

"Yes, there is! Is he dead or not?" Ollis yells.

"Ollis, calm down. What's the matter with you?" Her mum's voice is getting sterner and sterner, but Ollis won't back down now.

"Tell me!"

"Ollis, you're not the one who makes the decisions in this house!" her mum says, staring Ollis down.

"I hate you!"

It just slips out. She wants to take it back. To catch the words, shove them back in her mouth and swallow them. But she's said it now.

Her mum doesn't say anything. She just stands there for a moment before nodding, leaving the room and closing the door carefully behind her.

15

It's morning. A fly is bouncing desperately against
the window. Ollis has been awake for a while, but
she can't quite bring herself to get up. The fog in her
chest hasn't lifted, it's just kind of settled. Ollis doesn't
know if she can face her mum. She doesn't know what
she'd say to make up for what she said last night. She
just wants to slip out of the house unseen. She listens.
The buzzing from the fly at the window mingles with
the noise from downstairs. They're in the kitchen.
Ollis looks at her watch. She needs to get going if
she's going to get to where she left the pram sled by
eleven. Ollis gets up and gets dressed as quietly as she
can before picking up her bag and tucking the fourth
letter inside. The kitchen is right by the front door.
They're bound to hear her if she goes out that way.
She scans her room, trying to think of something
clever, but the fly is a bit distracting. Ollis puts her

hands over her ears, but it doesn't help.

"Argh!" Ollis sighs. She tiptoes over to the window and opens it. The fly bounces off the glass another four or five times before making it through the gap to freedom. Ollis is about to close the window again when she sees it. Gro's rope ladder! Quick as a flash, she clambers through the window and climbs down. On the ground, she crouches down and hurries around the side of the house. She checks whether the coast is clear across the yard. There's no one in sight. She starts running.

"Arf!" Micro yips at her from his little doghouse. He's standing to attention in the doorway.

"Shh!" Ollis hisses. Micro wags his tail and yips again.

Ollis speeds up and dives behind the trees. She looks back across the yard. No one seems to have seen her apart from Micro, who is gazing longingly at the forest. Ollis nods to herself. She's getting the hang of this.

The Goat of Christmas Past is no longer a concern. He knows what to expect when Ollis releases the ink cartridges now. Now he just cowers around the side of the farmhouse and snorts every time Ollis crosses the farmyard.

The forest is no longer unfamiliar. She knows every

rock and tuft of grass all the way from the farmyard to Borgny's cabin. She's there in no time. She doesn't even knock, just holds the fourth letter up in front of the window. She hears footsteps in the hall, and then the door opens.

Ollis goes in, gives Borgny the letter, collects the day's post from the kitchen table and carries it down into the basement. Borgny follows on her heels, coffee cup clattering on its saucer.

Ollis sits down on the basement floor, picks up the letter opener and gets to work on the envelopes. The first letter is for someone called Elisabeth. Ollis's mind wanders to her mum. She shouldn't have said she hated her. She should have said… something else. Something to make her realise how serious the situation is. Something to make her understand how upset Ollis is. Ollis slips the letter opener inside the envelope and slits it open. And another. And then another. She establishes a rhythm, opening the envelopes quickly and dumping their contents in Borgny's lap. Ten, twenty, thirty…

"Hey!" Borgny suddenly yells, snatching the letter opener out of Ollis's hand. "Cool your jets!"

She leans forward in her chair, brandishing the letter opener.

"I don't want it looking like the letters were opened by cows."

"Don't be daft," Ollis says, affronted.

"It's not daft. Cows have real trouble opening letters. No fingers, you see."

Borgny curls her fingers together so her hands look like hooves. Ollis rolls her eyes.

"I mean it's daft to care how the envelopes look. It's not like anyone except you will ever read what's in them."

Borgny looks at Ollis, tilting her head like Macro does when Ollis makes cat noises.

"Are you in a mood?"

"No, I'm not in a mood."

"Yes, you are."

"I'm not!" Ollis says.

"Sure looks like it." Borgny smirks and leans even further forward for a closer look.

Ollis turns away from her.

"Haha! You *are* in a mood!" Borgny says, laughing. "You're pretending not to be, but you can't fool me." Borgny applauds herself. "I'm very good at reading people."

Ollis makes the world's worst attempt at a smile and holds her hand out for the letter opener. Borgny gives it to her, leans back in her armchair again and slurps her coffee. Ollis keeps opening letters, only now she does it with exaggerated care before handing them reverently to Borgny, who is still watching her over the rim of her coffee cup.

"Why are you in a mood?" Borgny asks. Ollis sighs dejectedly.

"I'm not in a mood," she says.

"You are, I can tell."

"I'm…" Ollis hesitates. "I've just got something on my mind," she finally admits.

"Oh?" Borgny says, setting her cup down. "Did you forget to put the milk back in the fridge?"

"Eh?"

"Oh! Or did you tell your friends to stand on one leg while playing "Simon Says" and then wander off and forget about them only to find them still standing there on one leg a week later?"

"What?" Ollis gapes at Borgny, who seems to be entirely serious. "No," Ollis says.

"Okay," Borgny says, leaning back. "I just wondered because that happened to me once."

Ollis shakes her head in disbelief.

"No, I said something I regret."

"To who? To your whiny friend?"

"No. To my mum."

"Ohhh!" Borgny gives a dismissive wave of her hand. "Is that all? But she's your mum! She'll still love you whatever you said."

Ollis shakes her head.

"Not now."

Ollis has a lump in her throat again. Swallowing is almost impossible. Borgny gets up and walks along one of the rows of shelves. When she comes back, she's carrying a folder.

"Hey, let's swap for a bit," she says, gesturing towards the armchair.

Ollis gives Borgny a suspicious look.

"Come on! I want to open the envelopes for a while. My letter-opening muscles could do with a workout."

Borgny jabs her finger impatiently at the armchair. Ollis gets up and sits on it. It's so deep she almost falls down between the cushions.

"Right, take this," Borgny says, dumping the folder in Ollis's lap. She sinks even deeper into the chair. "And read."

Borgny plops down on the floor and starts opening envelopes. Ollis watches her. Is this a trick? What if she's just trying to find a reason to accuse Ollis of snooping so she can throw her out? Slowly, Ollis opens the folder. Borgny doesn't react, so Ollis starts reading the faded loopy handwriting on the first envelope.

"Filli Radenschnei," she says slowly.

When she looks up again, Borgny nods eagerly.

"It's my favourite folder!"

Ollis takes out the first letter. It's yellow and old. It was sent by a man called Jörg Efelsten. It's a love letter. *Denmark, 21 June 1964* is written in the top right-hand corner.

It seems that Jörg, the sender, has admired Filli for a long time and finally decided to tell her how he feels. The language is a bit flowery, but he's clearly trying to tell her that he's in love with her. He compares Filli to all sorts of beautiful things. A meadow in July, sunlight glittering on water, mountains after the first snow has fallen. Jörg ends the letter by saying it doesn't matter how she feels about him – what is most important is that she knows how he feels about her. Ollis thinks it's nice. Love with no strings or any expectation of anything in return. In his next letter, Jörg asks for a response from Filli. He writes that it needn't be a long response, just a hint about how she feels about him. It doesn't matter to him what she feels – he just wants to know whether it's good or bad. But then, in the letters that follow, Jörg becomes increasingly irritated about the lack of response from Filli. In one of them he curses her, telling her she's poison and that she has poisoned him. He apologises for this in the next letter. Then he changes his mind again. Although it's kind of sad, Ollis can't help but laugh. It's as if Jörg's arguing with himself. In his very last letter he comes to much the same realisation and says that this is the last letter he'll ever send Filli. He asks her to forgive him for wasting her time. Ollis puts the letter down and shakes her head. Borgny claps her hands together.

"Good, aren't they?"

"Yes," Ollis says, laughing again.

"You see how you're like Jörg, right? You see how silly you're being?"

"What? No!" Ollis says, perturbed.

"Jeez. You're really not the sharpest pencil in the box," Borgny says, putting her face in her hands. "Jörg thinks she's refusing to reply and is trying desperately to find out why! He comes up with hundreds of potential reasons why, but there's only one explanation: she doesn't know anything about the letters he's sent her. Because they've ended up here – in my letterbox!"

Ollis gives Borgny a quizzical look. Borgny sighs and spells it out for her, speaking very slowly and clearly.

"Have you actually tried asking your mum how she feels, or are you just torturing yourself by *imagining* how she feels?"

Ollis shrugs.

"That's what I like best about all these letters. Read enough of them and you realise we're all equally idiotic." Borgny smiles at Ollis. "I think it would be sensible to talk to your mum."

Ollis closes the folder and goes to put it back on the shelf. Is Borgny right? Can it be that her mum hasn't chosen Einar over Ollis? Is the whole thing one big misunderstanding?

"Done!" Borgny suddenly shouts. Ollis peers out from behind the shelves. Borgny is fanning herself with the pile of open letters.

Ollis takes them from her and starts putting them into their respective folders. Slowly but surely she files them all away until she only has one left. For someone called Halls. If only it were Haalsen instead. Ollis Haalsen. But nothing has come for Ollis today either. She walks over to the H shelves. Row six, right up against the wall. She peers at the top shelf where the H folders begin. Haga, Hagestad, Hakkerud, Halerud… Finally she spots the Halls folder. She takes it down and tucks the letter inside before reaching up to put it back.

That's when she sees it. The very first folder. Right at the top and right against the wall. The name written on it is so long it fills the entire spine from top to bottom. Ollis gasps. Her heart starts pounding. Faster and faster as she stares at the name. Oda… Lise… Louise… Sonja… Haalsen. Ollis blinks a couple of times to make sure she's not seeing things. But nothing changes. There's no doubt. She reaches for the folder, gripping the spine and pulling it towards her. It's thick and heavy. Too heavy, Ollis realises as it slides off the shelf. She loses her grip and suddenly it's raining postcards.

16

"Borgny!" Ollis yells, emerging from between the rows of shelves with her arms full of postcards. Borgny holds one of the folders up in front of her like a shield.

"Help!" she squeaks. Ollis stops right in front of her, nostrils flaring.

"You lied!" Ollis says, holding the pile of postcards out towards Borgny.

"What?" Borgny says, peering out from behind the folder. She looks confused.

"You said there hadn't been any post for me!"

"There hasn't."

"Then what's all this?!"

Borgny peers cautiously over the edge of the folder.

"Postcards!" she whimpers. "Is that the right answer? Don't hurt me." She raises the folder again.

"They're for me!"

"Are they?" Borgny tosses the folder aside and

snatches one of the postcards out of Ollis's hands.

"Haha. No, no, silly. These are for Oda. Lise. Louise. Sonja. Haalsen. Dearie me, bit of a mouthful, isn't it?"

Borgny gives Ollis a crooked smile.

"But that's what Ollis is short for! Don't you see?" Ollis jabs her finger at the long name. Borgny pats her shoulder, and when she speaks again, it's in the softest voice she can muster.

"Are you feeling quite alright?"

"Argh!" Ollis groans, slapping her hand away. She looks down at the postcards.

"Ingrid!" she says to herself before holding one of the postcards up for Borgny to see. "He's forgotten Ingrid. That's why they ended up here!"

Ollis can almost hear the cogs turning in Borgny's mind as she murmurs something quietly to herself.

"Wow. Well, that would make it Ollis," she says suddenly, laughing nervously. "But then aren't you… I'm sure you're absolutely… erm… delighted, then? That you've found the postcards? Not angry?"

Borgny fiddles with one of the buttons on her jacket. Ollis looks at the postcards in her hands. In truth, she couldn't be more delighted.

"Woohoo!" Ollis cheers, throwing her arms around Borgny's middle.

"Help!" Borgny shouts again.

The postcards are from all over the world. The pictures on the front are from China, Japan, Australia, Peru, Alaska, Kenya, Thailand, Italy. Ollis can't believe it. There are a hundred in total, and they're all for her. From Borgepa. He's alive!

Ollis sits in Borgny's kitchen with the postcards strewn over the floor. They all say almost the exact same thing.

Hi, Ollis. It's me. I love you. And then he's drawn a sailing boat. On every single one. It says Happy Birthday on some and Merry Christmas on others. It's still all very confusing, but the postcards make her happy. She can't remember the last time she was happy. Borgepa's out there, sailing from place to place, stopping to buy postcards whenever he goes ashore. At every single port he thinks of Ollis.

I love you, they say. A hundred times.

Ollis thinks about her mum. Maybe she doesn't know. She might not even know Borgepa's out there. Imagine how happy she'll be when she finds out he's not dead! Ollis's insides are fizzy with excitement. She wants to go home. She needs to go now. If she dares tell her mum the whole truth, everything might be okay. Maybe Ollis can have both her mum and Borgepa back again. Ollis shoves the postcards into her bag and heaves it onto her shoulders. Borgny is slumped on a kitchen chair, pretending to be asleep. She's been doing it for the last half an hour to get out of helping.

"I'll be back tomorrow!" Ollis says. Borgny doesn't open her eyes. She just gives Ollis a thumbs up and keeps pretending to snore. Ollis throws open the front door and realises straight away that it's later than usual. The light is completely different. She looks at her watch. Quarter past five. Billy Kapra will have been home for ages. Ollis runs through the forest. All the way to her pram sled, which she gets moving with a powerful kick against the gravel track. She can't lose her nerve now.

When Ollis reaches the edge of the birch forest, there are lights on at the goat farm. The chain hangs loosely from the farmhouse wall. Good. That means both Billy Kapra and the Goat of Christmas Past are in the goat shed. Ollis needs to make it to the other side of the farmyard before either of them come back out again. She can see a narrow opening behind the farmhouse, between the wall and the fence. Ollis kicks off and wrenches the pram sled to the right. She only just gets it turned around in time to zip behind the small, white building. Once she's in position she looks over at the combine harvester sitting by the barn. That's her target. But as she prepares to kick off again, the goat shed door opens. Ollis jumps and ducks back behind the farmhouse wall. She sees the light from the goat shed go out. Hears the gravel in the yard crunching under a man's wellies. The farmhouse door opens, the wellies are kicked against the threshold, and the door closes again with a click.

Ollis doesn't waste any time. She jumps on the pram sled and kicks off hard. But then, suddenly, a loud creaking noise cuts through the silence. It's coming from the wheels. Her heart pounds like a drum. The farmhouse door opens again. A beam of light sweeps slowly across the farmyard.

"Hello?" Billy Kapra's deep voice booms out.

Two seconds pass. Three. Four. Then the door creaks closed again. CLICK.

Ollis heaves a sigh of relief. If Billy Kapra had taken one more step out into the yard, he'd have seen her bag sticking out from behind the combine harvester. She quickly covers her mouth, fighting down an unexpected bubble of laughter.

Ollis more or less flies through the forest. To think she managed to sneak undetected across Billy Kapra's farmyard! She wishes she could tell Gro. Maybe she could tell her mum. She can start by apologising. She thinks that's the best thing to do, so her mum knows she doesn't hate her. Ollis can see the light from home through the trees now. She's so excited! Ollis jumps the last part of the path down into the yard and bounds towards the house.

Smiling, she kicks off her shoes in the hall. Then she hears something. What was that? Ollis listens. There's a sniff from the living room. Ollis takes off her jacket as quietly as she can so she can hear better.

"Yes," someone says, sounding tearful. It's her mum.

Ollis quickly takes off her bag and heads towards the living room, stopping in the doorway. Her mum looks up, her eyes shining with unshed tears. Einar is kneeling on the floor. Has she been telling Einar about what Ollis said?

"Er, sorry, I just-" Ollis says.

Her mum just shakes her head before smiling through her tears. She looks from Einar to Ollis before showing Ollis her hand. A small diamond sparkles on her finger.

"We're getting married!"

17

Ollis stands in the middle of her room staring into space. How could she have been so stupid? As if her mum would ever have chosen her over Einar. She can't stay here. Her mum doesn't even care that Ollis hates her. She needs to see Gro. She'll just say she's back from seeing Borgepa a day earlier than expected. Ollis grabs her bag and climbs out of the window and down the rope ladder.

The light is on in Gro's room. *It'll be so good to see her*, Ollis thinks. Her Gro, who always has something bizarre to say to cheer her up. Maybe she should tell her about Borgepa. Gro might understand if Ollis explains everything. About the postcards and about how she'd thought he was dead and about how Ollis had just been jealous of Gro when she'd said he was alive. Ollis goes through the white gate and walks over to the house, where she scoops up some small stones and starts throwing them up at Gro's window. First one, then two, then three – but nothing happens. *Ugh,* Ollis thinks. Gro doesn't have a rope ladder, so she'll have to knock. She's only been waiting a couple of seconds when she hears someone in the hall. Gro's dad opens the door.

"Ollis? We don't usually see you here this late."

Ollis tries to smile, but it doesn't quite reach her eyes.

"I just want to talk to Gro quickly," Ollis says.

"Sure," Gro's dad says. He starts to turn around again, but then pauses. "Um…" His eyes are worried, like Einar's when he can't work out why Ian's crying.

"Wait here a moment," Gro's dad says, going back inside. More than a moment passes, but eventually Gro appears in the hall.

"Ahoy-hoy," Gro says. She leaves it at that, frowning at Ollis.

"I need to tell you something insane," Ollis starts.

"Something insane like how you've *lied* to me?" The word is like a punch to Ollis's gut.

"What…" Ollis starts.

"How many times have I told you that camouflage is everything? Seems you completely forgot about that when you climbed down the rope ladder earlier today. I can see your bedroom window from mine."

Ollis's head is a mess. A tornado of lies and secrets she can't control anymore. She finds herself lying again even though she knows it's stupid.

"Borgepa was sick, so I…"

"Stop!" Gro stamps her foot. "Stop lying, Ollis! I know you don't have a dad! Dad told me. Admit you've been lying to me. You've been lying to me for years!"

Ollis suddenly aches all over.

"You lied even though I told you liars are the worst."

"Sorry, Gro, I-"

"Drop it. Just tell me where you've been."

Ollis looks at the ground. Gro lowers her voice.

"Have you been at Borgny's? Don't tell me you've been wasting your time with that twit."

Ollis swallows and swallows to stop herself from crying.

"Gro, I needed-"

"Are you for real!" Gro says, trying to slam the door in her face, but Ollis sticks her foot out to stop it.

"Gro, I'm sorry! You need to help me. Mum and Einar are getting married."

Then something completely unexpected happens. Gro opens the door again, leans out and pushes Ollis, with both hands, as hard as she can. It all seems to happen as if in slow motion. Ollis hits the ground hard. Her bag goes flying and skids along the gravel path.

"Tell them I said hello and congratulations," Gro says. She closes the door, and a second later Ollis hears the latch click.

Ollis doesn't make any move to get up. She just lies there. Alone. She wants to scream, but there's no point. No one can hear her. No one wants to hear her. There's no one left. Slowly, she sits up. The palm of her right hand is a bit scraped. She brushes off the worst of the gravel and picks up her bag. Some of the postcards from Borgepa fall out and land on the ground. Ollis picks them up.

Hi, Ollis! It's me. I love you.

Well, that's it, then, Ollis thinks. It's just the two of them now. Ollis *has* to find Borgepa.

She sprints back home. Climbs up the rope ladder and into her room. She opens her bag and pours the postcards onto the floor. Spreads them out using her hands so none of them are overlapping. It's the postmarks in the top right-hand corners she needs to see. The dates when the postcards were sent. She needs to know when he sent them and how long he's been sending them. Some of the postmarks are quite clear, but others have almost entirely faded. She orders the ones with postmarks she can read from oldest to most recent. After an hour, the line of postcards reaches from the door to her closet. An hour after that, it's past her desk. The line gets longer and longer and it gets later and later. Ollis lies on her front on the floor, trying to read the postmarks. She yawns. Her eyelids get heavy, but Ollis forces them open again. She can't sleep now. She just can't.

Ollis wakes with a start and sits up. It's morning. She reaches up to unstick a postcard from her cheek. It's the one with the most recent date on it. It's only a month old, from Thailand. All hundred postcards are lying picture side down. They cover Ollis's floor. The oldest postcard is from when Ollis was only one. Borgepa has been sending her postcards for ten years. Without knowing whether she's received any of them. But he'll find out soon. Ollis just needs to work out where he is. Ollis turns the postcards over one by one.

    Borgepa is an explorer, there's no doubt about that. He's been everywhere. There's a new country or a new town on every single postcard. Once she's turned them all over, she stands up so she can look at them all at once. But she doesn't even recognise half the places. She'll have to take them to Borgny's. Borgny is the only person who can help her now. Ollis gathers up the postcards and puts them in her bag together with Borgny's fifth and final letter.

18

When Ollis reaches the small house in the birch forest, Borgny is waiting for her at the door.

"It's about time," Borgny says.

"We're not opening post today," Ollis says, marching straight past her.

"Oh, but we are. That's your job," Borgny says shortly, stomping after her.

"You had a whole folder of postcards for me and didn't tell me."

Borgny throws her arms up in exasperation.

"How was that my fault? How on earth was I to know you're Oda Lise Louise Sonja when you introduce yourself as Ollis?" Borgny gives Ollis a reproachful look. "Be reasonable."

Ollis groans.

"Borgny, you knew I was looking for postcards. You owe me, and you know it," Ollis says sternly.

Borgny pouts.

"Oh, alright," she says after a couple of seconds, shuffling into the kitchen.

Ollis goes straight down into the basement. There, she pulls the postcards out of her bag and sorts them into piles. One pile for each year. Borgny comes down the stairs. Ollis can hear her coffee cup clinking.

"Here," Borgny says. Ollis looks up. Borgny is holding two cups and offering one to her.

"Lots of sugar," Borgny says, trying to wink. She almost manages it, her mouth twisting clumsily.

Ollis takes a sip of the coffee. It tastes awful, but the warmth that trickles down her throat is quite nice. It reminds her of drinking her mum's hot chocolate.

Borgny sits in the green armchair.

"Well?" she asks.

Ollis looks up from the piles on the floor.

"Well, what?"

"Did you talk to your mum yesterday?"

Ollis shakes her head and keeps sorting.

"Why not?"

"She was… busy," Ollis says.

"With what?"

"Something."

"What sort of something?"

"Nothing," Ollis says, irritated.

"But if it was nothing, she'd have had time to talk to you!"

"She's getting married, okay?" There's a pause before Borgny speaks again.

"Ew!" she says, wrinkling her nose. "Why would she do that?"

Ollis has to laugh.

"No idea."

The corners of her mouth droop again. She has a pretty good idea.

"Well, I guess..." she says. "I guess now she can have a proper family, you know? With a husband and a baby."

Borgny just stares at Ollis for a few seconds before bursting out laughing.

"That's the stupidest thing I've ever heard."

That's when Ollis's irritation turns to anger.

"Well, you're the stupidest person I've ever met!" she snaps.

Unfortunately, this makes Borgny laugh even harder. She slaps her thigh like she's just been told the funniest joke in the world.

"Sorry, but you really don't get it, do you? There's no such thing as a 'proper' family." Borgny gets up and walks over to the closest bookshelf. She points at a folder.

"This family has a mother and a father who live together."

Then she points at the next one along.

"The child in this family lives with his mother and his father lives elsewhere, but they're still a family."

She keeps pointing out different folders on various shelves.

"Here, two mothers. Here, two fathers. And believe it or not, there's no mother or father in this one. The children live with their grandparents."

Borgny crosses her arms and gives Ollis a triumphant look.

"All these families are proper families. A hundred per cent proper."

She lifts her head and gazes philosophically into thin air.

"The way I see it, your family's the people you love, and the people who love you."

Ollis looks at Borgny, standing there with her unruly curls and round glasses, completely alone. Maybe it's not so much she doesn't want to live in the village as she doesn't dare. However, Ollis only manages to feel sorry for Borgny for a couple of seconds before she ruins it.

"And I'm also a family because I love Borgny and Borgny loves me."

She nods demonstratively, as if to punctuate her speech.

Ollis doesn't answer. She doesn't want to talk about who is family and who isn't anymore. And she definitely doesn't want to be her own family. She puts the last postcard in its pile.

"What we need to do is work out whether Borgepa's taking any particular route or whether there are any connections between the places he visits. That way, we might be able to work out where he's going next."

"Borgepa?" Borgny asks.

"The man who sent me these postcards. He's been to a lot of places. So many I haven't even heard of half of them. That's why I need you to help me."

Borgny looks at Ollis. Opens her mouth as if to say something, but then closes it again. Then she gets up and goes upstairs.

"Borgny!" Ollis is so tired of Borgny's erratic behaviour. "Borgny! I need you to help me!" But Borgny disappears through the trapdoor without a word. Frustrated, Ollis slams her fist against the floor. Then there's a crash from upstairs, like something's fallen over. Everything is silent for a moment.

"Eureka!" Borgny shouts. She comes staggering down the basement steps with a huge book in her hands.

"I knew there was an atlas at the bottom of one of those piles of books."

She lifts the book triumphantly over her head before throwing herself down on the floor next to Ollis. They get started.

Ollis reads the names of the places and Borgny looks them up. Borgny laughs when Ollis can't pronounce some of them. But Ollis doesn't get annoyed. In fact, she laughs as well. Some of the place names are really hard. Names like Tegucigalpa, Ljubljana and Ngerulmud.

Borgepa really has been all over the world, to the biggest cities and remotest villages, but it's difficult to find a pattern. He sometimes travels from a country in the West straight to one on the other side of the world. And then to somewhere very near the first place. It's like he's just closing his eyes and sticking a pin in a map to pick his destinations. The more places they find, the more difficult it gets to work out where he might go next. By the time Borgny's looking up the last city, Ollis is more confused than ever.

"Well…" Borgny says. "Do you see any… pattern?" She gives Ollis a somewhat anxious smile.

Ollis just sits there holding the final postcard.

"It's a bit of a haphazard way to travel," Borgny says hesitantly.

Ollis doesn't reply. She can feel her eyes prickling again. *Don't cry,* she thinks, blinking the tears away. But if she can't find Borgepa, she's on her own. All alone. She jumps as Borgny suddenly starts patting her on the head with one of her large hands. It's a bit on the forceful side, but if the words that follow are any indication, she's trying to be comforting.

"There, there. I know."

Ollis clears her throat and stands up.

"I should really get going."

She pulls her bag towards her and starts picking up postcards from the floor and shoving them inside. Borgny scoops up a handful.

"It says he loves you here," Borgny says, smiling encouragingly and showing her one of the postcards. Ollis nods and tries to smile, but she just can't anymore. Borgny sighs and looks back at the postcard. Then, as Ollis rakes up the remaining postcards from the floor, she suddenly cries out.

"WAIT!"

She waves the postcard frantically as she flicks through the others she picked up. Soon there are postcards flying everywhere. When she runs out, she grabs some more from Ollis and starts flicking through those as well.

Then she shoves her arm into Ollis's bag and pulls out the rest.

"Hey!" Ollis says, irked. But Borgny's not listening. She's too busy throwing postcards around. Ollis gets down on all fours and starts scooping them up again. The same postcards she spent a whole night putting in order.

"Oh, oh!" Borgny shouts. She looks at Ollis and points at the only postcard still in her hand. "He's having you on!"

She grabs Ollis's hands to get her attention and throws her arms in the air.

"Don't you see?" Borgny asks frantically. She drops to the floor and seizes some more of the postcards. She points at the postmarks.

"Borgny! We've already gone through the dates. They didn't-"

"No!" Borgny says, waving her arms around some more. "Not the date. The place." She taps one of the postmarks and holds the postcard out for Ollis to have a closer look. Then she sees what Borgny means. The postmark says Hamna.

"That's where the postcard was sent from," Borgny whispers. "And it says Hamna on all of them."

19

Ollis can't believe it. Her absent father, a man she wasn't even sure was alive, is in *Hamna*? Hamna, the town only half an hour away by car? Has he been there the whole time? And if he has, why hasn't he visited her? Or called? Does her mum know? Is she the one who stopped him visiting? Ollis has so many questions that her brain feels like soup.

"Hello?" Borgny waves a hand in front of Ollis's face.

"What? Oh," Ollis says. "I… I need to go." Ollis stuffs all the postcards into her bag, closes it and throws it over her shoulders before heading upstairs.

"You're going?" Borgny asks incredulously, grabbing the coffee cups and hurrying after her. "Well, then," she says shrilly. "This is the last time you'll walk up these stairs."

Ollis strides purposefully across the bedroom.

"The last time you'll be in this bedroom." Borgny follows on Ollis's heels.

"The last time you'll walk along this hall-" Ollis whirls around and Borgny crashes into her.

"Oof!"

Ollis looks at Borgny. Her small eyes magnified by her round glasses. Her wild, curly hair and strange behaviour.

"Thanks for your help," Ollis says, wrapping her arms around her waist. Borgny goes rigid. She turns red, her eyes darting here and there. Then she brings the two coffee cups to her lips and downs the last few drops.

"Mmm. Yum," she says, most of it running down her chin. "Cold coffee!"

Ollis smiles, opens the front door and waves one last goodbye. Borgny is a bit odd, but she's alright.

Ollis makes the trip home with a thousand thoughts swirling in her head. If Borgepa is in Hamna, that means she's actually managed to find him. Just like she wanted to. But that's almost scarier than not knowing where he is. Could she actually visit him? What if he's not there anymore? What if he lived there for ten years but decided to leave a week ago? Then she'd have nowhere to go. Then she'd really be all alone. And how would she get there? She's never been that far away from home on her own before. And sure, it only takes half an hour to drive, but it would take at least five hours to walk. Ollis is so lost in her thoughts that she's surprised to find herself suddenly back at the house.

"Hi." Einar is standing in the yard with the dogs' food bowls in his hands. "Where've you been?"

Ollis is so bewildered she forgets to lie.

"The birch forest."

"Are you allowed in there?"

Ollis doesn't reply.

"I won't say anything if you don't," he says in a low, conspiratorial voice, trying to wink. Light reflects off his greasy glasses. Ollis needs him to keep it to himself, so she forces a grateful smile.

"In you come, then," Einar says. "We need a little help in here."

Ollis goes into the hall and takes off her shoes. Einar tries to help her with her bag.

"No," Ollis yelps, wrapping her arms around it. Alarmed, Einar takes a step back.

"I just… I'm taking it up to my room," Ollis says, her heart pounding. Her mum emerges from the living room.

"Hi, sweetie. Come in here a moment," she says, ushering Ollis inside. "We need help writing the invitations."

Ollis tries to squirm away, but her mum steers her all the way over to the table and pushes her down onto a chair. The table is covered in envelopes and cards and pens and ribbons. Ollis sniffs.

"Could you please," her mum says, bringing her hands together, "just this once, behave like your old self and help us out?"

Ollis wants to push everything onto the floor and yell that it's her mum who needs to behave like her old self, but she knows she'll start crying if she does that, so she just turns towards the table and picks up a black pen.

"Thank you," her mum says. "If you could write the name-"

Her mum is interrupted by an ill-tempered howl from upstairs.

"Oh, someone's hungry," she says, hurrying from the room. Einar comes in from the hall like he was hiding out there. He peers over the top of his glasses at Ollis.

"You know what you're doing?" Ollis fiddles with the pen and shakes her head.

"It's nothing too complicated. We've already written the invitations. We just thought it'd be nice if you wrote the names and addresses on the envelopes." Einar picks up some sheets of paper and gives them to Ollis. It's a list of all the addresses.

"We need to get them sent out as soon as possible. After all, the wedding's in September."

He laughs his stupid clucking laugh. Ollis pulls one of the invitations towards her, slowly.

"Good stuff!" Einar says, shuffling into the kitchen. Ollis opens the invitation and reads it.

The Haalsen/Strøm family
invite you to celebrate the wedding of
Elisabeth and Einar on 4 September at 1 pm.
We hope you can make it!

I don't, Ollis thinks. Her mum has signed the bottom of the invitation in her soft round handwriting. Einar has signed it in handwriting so jagged it looks more like he's drawn a mountain range. Ollis moves her thumb to find that someone has signed Ian's name as well. She moves her whole hand, but there's nothing more to see. She picks up another invitation, but they're all the same. Ollis's name isn't written on any of them. They haven't included her.

Einar appears in the doorway.

"Good job, Ollis! Everyone needs to help out in this family, you know!"

But it's clear to Ollis that she isn't part of this family. There's no fog in her chest or lump in her throat this time – it's more like a black veil has been drawn over her. As Einar goes into the kitchen, Ollis starts shoving invitations into envelopes and scribbling addresses at breakneck speed, all without looking at the list Einar gave her. She makes up first names, surnames, street names, everything. None of the invitations have the right address on them. Her mum and Einar can celebrate their stupid wedding on their own. She almost wishes she could see their faces when they're standing all dressed up in church waiting for their guests and none of them show up. But by the time the fourth of September comes, Ollis will be far, far away. What was it Borgny said? Your family's the people you love, and the people who love you. Fine, then Ollis will go to her family. To the person who's written 'I love you' a hundred and one times. It's time to find Borgepa.

20

Later in the evening, once Ollis has finished writing the wrong names on all the envelopes, she smiles sweetly and tells her mum and Einar that she'll post them as well. They're delighted, gushing about how kind she is. If only they knew. Ollis runs up to her room with all the invitations in a plastic bag. She tosses it on her bed, walks over to her bedside table and picks up her tablet. She searches for aerial images of the area, finding a lovely big picture of their village and Hamna. Ollis zooms in. She can see the road winding between houses and around the forests and mountains. And she's right – walking along the road would take much too long, even if she used her pram sled. But what about…? Ollis leans closer. The river flowing past Billy Kapra's farm and into the birch forest leads to Hamna, and that route would be three times shorter than the road. At least. But even though it would only take Ollis two or three hours to walk that way, she'd still need a head start. Ollis usually gets up at nine, so her mum probably won't check her room before ten. Maybe eleven. And then she'll check whether Ollis is at Gro's, and that will take half an hour. As long as Ollis and Borgepa have left Hamna by noon, no one will find them. She'll need to walk while it's still dark so she gets to Hamna early tomorrow. Now she just needs to figure out how to get through the forest in the dark. She'll need to take the ink cartridges with her so she can scare away the Goat of Christmas Past and other wild animals. But what she needs most is light. A torch won't be enough in the birch forest for someone as afraid of the dark as Ollis. She needs something bigger.

"Light, light, light," Ollis mumbles to herself as she wanders around her room, picking up things that might be useful. She opens her bedside drawer. It's full of screws and nails and glue as well as door handles and those tiny light bulbs you use for fairy lights. Fairy lights! Ollis slams the drawer closed again and walks over to the hooks on the back of her door. She takes down her fairy light umbrella, switches off the main light and opens it. It lights up Ollis, but not a lot more. It's too small. She'll need to make a new one. A bigger one.

She has four hours.

Ollis runs out to the garage. She slithers around the creaky door and starts clearing the shelves of headlamps, torches, bike lights... every type of light she can find that runs on batteries. Then she reaches for the box of Christmas decorations and pulls it down from the shelf. She stumbles slightly under the weight of it, but quickly regains her balance and manages to put it down on the ground without dropping it. She opens it and pulls out all the fairy lights she can find. She's about to put it back when she spots something else up there – her mum's huge, rainbow-coloured umbrella. Ollis climbs up onto the bottom shelf, straining to reach it. Eventually she manages to grab its curved handle and pull it towards her. The umbrella is almost as long as Ollis is tall. She opens it carefully. It goes up slowly, springing out with a *whumph!* and revealing all its colours. Ollis holds it above her head and spins it around. It's so big she could use it as a boat if she turned it upside down. She could even bring a friend. If she had one. Ollis finds some tape and string and gets to work.

Three hours later, Ollis is back in her room contemplating a small collection of items on her floor. Green jacket, green hat, wellies with foliage for camouflage purposes, and her bag, which is now full of clothes. She's put the postcards from Borgepa in her safe. She doesn't need them anymore. But she *has* packed the old photo of the two of them. The umbrella, now all kitted out, lies on top of everything else. The plastic bag full of invitations and her old fairy light umbrella are there too. After all, she did say Gro could have it when she died. Ollis isn't intending to die on this trip, but she'll probably never see Gro again. From now on, it's just Ollis and Borgepa. Ollis checks the time. It's eleven o'clock. There's only one more thing she needs to do before she leaves. Ollis goes into the bathroom and grabs her mechanical toothbrush. Then she crosses the hall to the door with the pillowy letters spelling I-A-N. She opens it carefully, getting ready to avoid the creaky floorboards, but then something makes her jump.

"Hi," her mum whispers. She's sitting on a chair by Ian's cot. Ollis starts to turn around, but her mum waves her inside, so she tiptoes over.

"I didn't think you'd still be up," her mum says quietly. Ollis nods and looks down at Ian, whose eyelids are drooping. She glances over at her mum. This feels like the first time they've been alone together in months.

"He's so peaceful," her mum says. Ollis just nods again. "Were you checking whether he was still awake?"

"No," she says. "I just wanted to say goodbye."

Her mum gives her a quizzical look.

"Goodnight! I meant… goodnight." Ollis feels her face flush. "And I wanted to give him this."

She lifts the mechanical toothbrush.

"You're giving him your tooth-brushing thing?" her mum asks, surprised. "You don't want to wait until he's awake?" Her mum looks at Ian and then back at Ollis again. "Or a bit older?" she adds, smiling.

Ollis shakes her head and sets it down on the chest of drawers.

"Are you okay, Ollis?" her mum asks, leaning forward slightly. Ollis quickly turns to face the door. She doesn't dare speak. She's afraid she'll just end up sobbing. She knows that if this had been before – before Einar, before Ian and before the postcards from Borgepa – she would have climbed onto her mum's lap and put her arms around her neck and everything would have been fine. But things weren't like that anymore, and they never would be ever again. So Ollis just nods her head again.

"Hmm, okay," her mum says, unconvinced.

"Goodnight, then. See you tomorrow."

Ollis doesn't want to turn around while there are tears in her eyes, so she just leaves the room and closes the door behind her.

21

Ollis climbs down the rope ladder for the last time. Darts across the yard for the last time. Her big green jacket is all done up, her hat pulled down over her forehead and pink hair. Her bag is on her back with the big umbrella wedged between it and her body. She stops down by the road and puts all the wedding invitations in the red postbox. Then she crosses the road to Gro's. She pauses for a moment by the white fence. There are no lights on in the narrow wooden house. Ollis takes the smaller umbrella out of her bag and hangs it from the gatepost. She looks up at the highest window and raises her hand in farewell.

"Goodbye, Gro," she whispers. Then she turns and leaves.

To make sure no one sees her from home or from Billy Kapra's farm, Ollis won't be able to use the umbrella until she's well into the birch forest.

She's only going to use a small headlamp on the path behind the house. It's too dark for Ollis, really, but it helps that she's walked the path so many times before. And at least the lamp gives her a little light. All the same, she feels like someone is watching her. Someone deep in the darkness. Ollis knows it's not possible to tell whether someone's watching you, but that doesn't stop the feeling. She hurries on. She just wants to get to her pram sled. Then she hears a snapping sound. Ollis whirls around, her heart pounding. What was that? She tries to look further down the path, but the light from her headlamp doesn't reach that far. Ollis shakes her head. If there's one thing she doesn't need to do on this trip, it's scare herself. She needs to calm down. She can't chicken out now. *I'm in a forest, and twigs snap in forests*, Ollis thinks, taking a deep breath. Then she starts walking again. A bit faster now. Luckily, she soon reaches the clearing where she left her pram sled.

Ollis pulls two big torches out of her bag and attaches them to the front of the pram sled. Hey presto – headlights. She turns the pram sled towards the forest and switches them on. Then she jumps. Did she just see someone duck behind a bush? *Calm down*, Ollis chides herself. *Calm down.* The headlights provide good light. Along with the umbrella it'll be just enough. She switches them off again. She can't have them on when she crosses the farmyard. She pushes the pram sled out of the clearing and kicks off, but she hasn't gone far when the pram wheels start to creak ominously. The closer she gets to the farm, the louder the noise. Ollis stops the pram sled and tips it onto its side. She peers between the wheels, but it's too dark to see anything. She can't turn on the lights while she's out in the open. Ollis rights the pram sled again and tries rolling it carefully onwards. By the time she reaches the barn, the creaking has become a constant screech. Ollis peers around the corner and across the farmyard. She can't back out now. Ollis puts her hand in her pocket, feeling the photo of her and Borgepa between her fingertips. She closes her eyes and pictures his crooked smile, the gap between his teeth and his smiling eyes. That's where she's going. Ollis lets out a ragged breath, grips the pram sled handlebar and starts jogging towards the farmyard. Once she's round the corner, she jumps up onto the pram sled. The screeching is worse than ever, but Ollis kicks off with as much strength as she can. Her momentum is good. The sound gets louder and louder, but she's halfway there. Ollis leans forward and smiles triumphantly. She's flying along. She's going to make it! But just as she's thinking this, the pram sled judders and stops dead, flipping Ollis over the handlebar. She hits the gravel so hard and fast that her body is dragged along the ground a short distance before she stops. Ollis shakes her head to collect her thoughts. She manages to stagger to her feet, but she can tell that her face and hands are all scraped. She tries to brush away the worst of the gravel and dirt. It really stings. Ollis hurries over to the pram sled. The pram wheels have completely buckled. She throws herself on the ground and tries to bend them back into shape. Then she hears someone at the farmhouse door. Moments later, it flies open. Ollis isn't able to run before the light from the hall hits her and the pram sled. She hides her face. She's rooted to the spot, unable to move. Billy Kapra comes stomping down the steps and out into the farmyard.

"What on earth is that-" he starts, before cutting himself off with a loud "Ouch!" He raises his hand to the back of his head and turns away from Ollis. She gets to her feet and sprints into the forest.

Ollis runs. She runs until her chest feels tight and her thighs ache. Away from her pram sled and what just happened with Billy Kapra in the farmyard. She doesn't dare stop until she's on the gravel track. The one that leads to the bottomless lake and then on to Borgny's. The path to Borgny's used to really scare Ollis, but now it feels safe. She wishes that was the path she was taking now, but it isn't. She's going right, following the path along the river. A narrow, unfamiliar path. It'll take her much longer now she doesn't have her pram sled. Best get going. Ollis grabs the umbrella strapped to her back, pulls it out like a lance and opens it. A tiny explosion of light cuts through the deep darkness, surrounding Ollis and lighting up the path. She grips the handle firmly and starts walking.

22

Ollis has decided she's not going to look right or left. It's so light under the umbrella that the forest seems extra dark and, for that reason, extra scary. Ollis walks as fast as she can, looking straight ahead. The plan was to have the ink cartridges from the pram sled with her to scare animals away, but she left them in Billy Kapra's farmyard. So here she is, walking and singing the soppiest song she knows to scare away elks and badgers.

"Give me your hand, my friend, as evening draws in and darkness descends."

Ollis sings as loudly as she can without drowning out the sound of the river. Any louder than that and she won't be able to hear anyone or anything sneaking up on her. Ollis can only remember the first verse, but it's better than nothing.

"Let happy thoughts follow us into sleep. Let the

warmth from someone who loves you shine like a star in the darkness. Give me your hand, my friend, as evening draws in and darkness descends."

Once Ollis has walked a fair distance and finished the first verse for the twentieth time, the song is interrupted by an insistent rumbling from her stomach. She stops and checks her watch. It's half past one. If her calculations are correct, she's walked about a third of the way to Hamna. If she had the pram sled, she'd be over halfway there. Ollis quickly shrugs off her bag. She pulls a bottle of juice out of one side pocket and takes a big gulp. Then she opens the other side pocket and digs out a packet of biscuits. She takes two from the packet before putting it back. She needs to ration her supplies. To make sure she has enough for the whole trip. As she starts to take her hand out of her bag again, she feels something. Her pedometer. It must have switched itself on when she was packing because it says she's walked just under three kilometres. The limit her mum set. The one Ollis has ignored several times in recent weeks. But that was different. Those times she was just walking the final two metres to Borgny's house. And Gro was with her. Ollis clenches her fist around the pedometer before putting her bag back on and shoving a biscuit in her mouth. She starts walking, picking up the pace. She watches the pedometer as it slowly but surely approaches the three-kilometre mark. 2.7, 2.8, 2.9. She starts running. She runs along the path as fast as she can. She runs until there's a stabbing pain in her chest. Until she can taste blood. She runs and runs until her right foot gets caught on a tree root. She goes flying, letting go of the pedometer, which is swallowed up by the darkness between the trees. Ollis props herself up on her elbows and gasps for breath. She tries to work out whether she's hurt. She's not, so she gets up. She doesn't bother brushing the dirt from her knees. Nor does she bother looking for the pedometer in the undergrowth. She's not on her mum's side anymore. From now on it's Ollis and Borgepa. Two loners with gaps between their front teeth, sailing away from all their troubles so they can be happy for the rest of their lives. Ollis wonders whether Borgepa likes inventing and making things too. Maybe they could do it together, as a father–daughter inventor duo renowned throughout Norway, or even throughout Europe! Then her mum will be sorry she chose Idiot Einar. He's not renowned for anything. She'll cry every time she sees Ollis and Borgepa in the news. She'll call at weekends, but Ollis will never pick up. She'll regret it for the rest of her life, all while Ollis and Borgepa sun themselves on their boat and cook sausages in the toaster and laugh themselves silly.

Ollis has been walking for a long time now. The path isn't always easy to see. Her shoes are starting to rub at her heels, and even though she has drunk almost all of her juice, her bag feels heavier than ever. She's so tired. Utterly exhausted. She can't even walk properly. Her feet drag on the path no matter how much she tries to lift them. She's dizzy too, and her head feels heavy. *What if I can't do this?* Ollis thinks. Why did she ever think this was a good idea? What if she's wandered off the path? Or what if Borgepa isn't in Hamna? She might be alone forever. What if a badger attacks her and bites her until her leg snaps and she can't walk anymore and dies out here? It's so dark, and she keeps thinking she can hear footsteps in the undergrowth and twigs snapping all over the place. Then, suddenly, something makes her stop. All her hair stands on end. There's someone on the path up ahead of her. Just standing there, watching her. Her heart is pounding so hard she can hardly hear herself when she speaks.

"Hello?"

No response. All Ollis can hear is her own heartbeat and the river. She drops down as quickly as she can, grabs a stone and hurls it at the figure, but they don't budge an inch.

"What do you want?" she yells. Still no response.

"Arghhh!" Ollis howls desperately into the darkness. She stomps her feet, her umbrella tilting back with the agitated movement so that the light projects further ahead. That's when she realises what she's looking at. It's just a stupid tree stump. Ollis lets herself slump down onto the forest floor like a sack of potatoes. She puts her arms over her face. She wants to sleep. For the rest of her life. To sleep until she's all grown up and not afraid anymore, and doesn't need anyone, and knows where she's going. She's had enough.

Ollis lies on the forest floor with her arms over her face for a long time. So long she wonders whether she's slept, but then she hears a noise. She moves her arms away from her face and sits up. A real noise. Not her imagination this time. What was that? It sounded like a whistle. *Fwheeooo, fwheeoooo.*

"Ugh," Ollis moans, lying down again. It's just a stupid bird. Wait, hold on… a bird? Ollis sits bolt upright again. What's a bird doing up in the middle of the night? She gets up. Was that it again? There are two of them. Three. She turns to her right and peers through the trees.

Ollis gasps as she sees the light on the crest of a distant hill. It's morning. She's done it – she's made it through the night! More and more birds join the morning chorus, and it's like they're cheering her on. *You can do it, you can do it!* The sun rises in slow motion and the forest thins out. Ollis keeps walking, finally breaking out into the open at the top of a hill. When she looks down, she can see Hamna. The early morning sun has made it over the crest of the hill and is bathing the harbour in glowing pink light. Ollis picks her way carefully down towards Borgepa.

23

The pink light soon becomes a warm orange that fills
every nook and cranny of Hamna.

Ollis sits on a green bench in front of a little red
boathouse looking out at the boats moored in the
harbour. There are twenty-five of them. Ollis has
counted them several times. Twenty smaller boats and
five sailing boats. And three empty moorings. There's
no one in any of the smaller boats, but there might be
in the sailing boats. Ollis had felt brave when she first
came out of the forest, but now she's been sitting here
for an hour trying to work up the courage to knock
on the doors of the five sailing boats to find out who
lives on them. Ollis dimly wonders whether she might
have switched her courage on too soon and used it
all up. She opens her bag and takes out the packet of
biscuits. She shakes the last one and some crumbs
into her hand. *Well rationed*, she thinks, taking a bite.
She's about to put the empty packet back into her

bag when she hears sounds coming from the closest sailing boat. The door to the cabin opens and a man ducks through. Ollis quickly looks away. But what if it's Borgepa? She looks again. Her eyes are fixed on him, watching every move he makes, but it's difficult to see his face. She gets up from the bench for a better view, but as she does, the man looks right at her. She doesn't know what to do, so she just looks back down at the bench again and pretends to be fascinated by the empty biscuit packet. Is he Borgepa? She couldn't quite tell.

"Hi there!" the man calls from the boat. Ollis pretends not to hear. What if he is Borgepa? What should she say? She doesn't look up, but she hears him jump ashore and start walking towards her. She sits stock still. He stops right in front of the green bench.

"Hi," he says again. Ollis doesn't respond.

"Are you waiting for someone?"

Ollis gives in to the urge to move. She looks up, but the sun dazzles her, making it difficult to see his face. He lifts his hand to shade her eyes. The man has short dark hair and glasses. He smiles. He doesn't have a gap between his front teeth. She nods.

"Alright," he says. "Are you sure?"

"Yes," Ollis says, looking down again.

"Looks like you've been in the wars," the man says, tapping his jaw.

"Oh," Ollis says, raising a hand to her own jaw. She doesn't know what it looks like after her tumble at Billy Kapra's, but she can feel there's a cut there.

"Yes, I fell. But I'm okay," Ollis says quickly, smiling.

"Okay, as long as you're sure," the man says, turning to leave.

"Wait," Ollis says. She puts the biscuit packet aside and rummages in her pocket. She pulls out the picture of her and Borgepa.

"Do you know who this is?" she asks, holding it out to him.

He shakes his head.

The sun climbs higher and higher in the sky. A family emerges from the second sailing boat and a young woman from the third. None of them recognise the man in Ollis's picture. Only two sailing boats left. It's eight o'clock. Ollis is still sitting by the boathouse. She's taken off her hat and unzipped her jacket. She's no more than twenty metres away from any of the boats, but it feels much further. Ollis closes her eyes. *If anyone comes up on deck before I've counted to five, I don't have to go and knock*, she thinks. *One, two,*

three… Ollis cracks one of her eyes open slightly. …
Four, four and a half, four and three quarters… five.
Ollis opens both eyes. Both the harbour and the decks
of the boats are deserted. Ollis picks up her bag and
umbrella and walks towards the last two sailing boats.
Her legs are like lead, but at least they're moving. The
boats are moored next to each other, but they're polar
opposites. One of them is white and really big. The
other is small and made of wood. Ollis decides to start
with the white boat. She walks over and raps on the
deck. No response. She tries again, but still nothing.
She clambers aboard and walks over to the cabin. She
lifts her fist, takes a deep breath and knocks on the
door. No reaction. She knocks again. Silence. That's
when she starts hammering on the door with the palm
of her hand until it shakes on its hinges.

"Oi!" a gravelly voice bellows from the
neighbouring boat. "There's no one home!"

Ollis jumps and presses herself against the door in
the hope that she won't be seen, but no such luck.

"I can see you! If you don't stop making that racket
I'll chuck you in the sea."

The door of the neighbouring boat slams and all
is quiet again. Ollis's heart has skipped at least ten
beats, but now it starts pounding again – so hard

it hurts. Billy Kapra's got nothing on this guy when it comes to being scary. But he's her final chance to find out anything about Borgepa. If she were Gro, she'd just barge in. Ollis clenches her fist around the umbrella. She can use it as a weapon if she has to. As she approaches the wooden boat where the angry man lives, she realises it's not only old, but also very run down. All the paint has flaked off the mast, and the wooden railing around the deck has started to rot in a few places. *That might be a good thing*, Ollis thinks. *This guy might have been here long enough to have met Borgepa.* She climbs carefully over the railing. There are some steps leading down to the cabin. Ollis is about to knock on the railing when she remembers what the man said about chucking her in the sea.

"Hello?" she tries cautiously, holding her umbrella out in front of her in case he suddenly bursts through the door. But he doesn't, so she tries again.

"Hello?" she says a bit louder, but nothing happens. Ollis tiptoes down the stairs, her heart trying to leap into her mouth. She grips the door handle and opens it.

It's dark inside the tiny cabin. So dark she can't see anything at first. But then, after a moment, her eyes start to adjust and the outline of a kitchen counter emerges from the gloom. It's laden with dirty dishes, used milk cartons and empty bottles. She can't see the man.

"Hello?" she tries again.

"What do you want?" the rough voice suddenly asks.

"I just wanted to ask you something, then I'll go."

The man snorts in response.

Ollis isn't entirely sure he's giving her permission, but she opens the door all the way and steps inside. The walls are covered in huge blue navigational charts. Photos from beaches and ports have been tacked up here and there. Ollis lets her eyes wander around the small room. It's not just the kitchen counter that needs cleaning. There's stuff all over the place. Old newspapers, dirty socks, dirty glasses and coffee cups full of cold coffee. There's a smell of sour milk and something Ollis can't quite place. Something sweet. She can just make out the man at the far end of the dark, narrow room. His hair is standing on end and he only has two of his shirt buttons done up. Both his elbows are on the table. He's hunched over, two huge fists around a coffee cup.

"You live here?!" Ollis exclaims without thinking.

The man clears his throat.

"Was that your burning question?" he asks.

"Oh. No, that's something else," Ollis says.

"I think it's best you leave. This is no place for kids," the man says.

"But it's just a quick question!" Ollis says, fumbling in her pocket for the picture. "I was just wondering-"

"Did you not hear what I said?" the man rumbled.

Ollis is terrified, but she can't back down now. She holds out the picture.

"Could you just look at this-"

"Are you deaf?" The large man gets up. He comes forward, and before Ollis can run or do anything else, he grabs hold of her shoulder.

"I said I think it's best you leave."

But Ollis can't move. She's rooted to the spot. She can't even remember how to breathe.

The man has a gap between his front teeth.

"Borgepa?" she asks quietly.

The man stops and looks at her. Right in the eyes. Ollis recognises them even though they're not smiling, like they are in the picture.

"Is your name Borge?" Ollis asks.

He lets go of Ollis's shoulder and takes a step back.

"I don't know you," he says, putting a hand on the table to steady himself.

"It's me. Ollis," Ollis says, smiling up at his craggy

face. It feels like there are a thousand butterflies in her stomach. She's found him. She did it. She did the scariest thing she could imagine, and now she's here – with Borgepa.

"I only just got all your postcards. All a hundred and one of them. From all over the world!" Words gush out of Ollis. "Have you been everywhere? In this boat? Have you been there?" She points at the wall, at the photograph with the bluest sea. "Can we go there? Can this boat still sail? I don't know much about sailing, but I want to learn. I want to be as good as you! Where can I sleep?"

Borgepa gapes at her.

"It's me!" Ollis says, pointing at the gap between her front teeth. "Oda Lise Louise Ingrid Sonja Haalsen."

He lets go of the table, bringing his big hands to his mouth. *Any second now he'll throw his arms around me*, Ollis thinks, *just like on TV when people see each other again after years and years apart.* She relaxes her arms, getting ready to hug him back. But he doesn't lunge forward to sweep her off her feet. He just looks away.

"It's me," Ollis says again, reaching out for him.

He clears his throat and shakes his head.

"I don't know what you mean," he says, starting to clear used coffee cups from the table.

"I got your postcards," Ollis says.

Borgepa walks over to the kitchen counter and puts the cups down without saying a word. He stands with his back to Ollis. The butterflies in her stomach simmer down.

Why isn't he answering?

"I only just got them. They ended up in the wrong place, you see. You forgot to write Ingrid."

Borgepa keeps cleaning the cups and plates from the counter. Ollis is starting to get irritated. No, not irritated… angry. She puts her hand in her pocket and pulls out the photo, shoving it between Borgepa and the sink.

"Look!" she says, waving the picture in his face. "I know this is you!"

He pushes her hand away.

"Listen," he says, still not turning around. "It's best you leave."

Ollis shakes her head in confusion.

"No," she says.

He says nothing.

"I walked all night. Don't you get it?! I'm ten years old and I walked all the way through the forest on my own to find you!"

"Like I said: this is no place for children."

"I don't have anywhere else to go!"

He sighs so deeply that his broad back strains against his shirt. Then he clears his throat.

"I…" He coughs slightly. "I'm no father. I can't-"

"You don't have to do anything," Ollis says. "We just need to love each other."

Borgepa gives a strange little croak. He drops a load of cups in the sink with a clatter.

"Please leave," he says gruffly.

"No," Ollis says.

"I can't take care of you!"

"You don't need to!" Ollis gestures impatiently. "I can look after myself! I could even help you. I can tidy, and wash up, and-"

Borgepa turns to face her. Without looking her in the eye, he grips her shoulders and pushes her towards the door. "Go!" he booms.

"No!" Ollis uses all her strength to resist him. Borgepa tries to push her back, but he's unsteady on his feet and she manages to twist out of his grip. He stumbles against the wall. Ollis lifts her fist and punches him in the side.

"You love me!" she howls. "I know you do!" Her voice cracks.

Borgepa buries his face in his hands and turns to

face the wall. Ollis doesn't move from the doorway.

Her heart is pounding in her chest and she's breathing heavily.

"It doesn't matter to me that you haven't been around." A big lump of nothing forces its way up into her throat, tearing at it like a jagged stone. Borgepa doesn't move, but Ollis can see his big body shaking. She swallows, lifts her hand and cautiously smoothes it across his broad back.

"You get to choose again," Ollis says quietly to the grown man hiding behind his hands. Borgepa sighs deeply again before shaking his head. Ollis takes back her hand, tears the photo into tiny pieces and throws them at him. Then she runs up the steps as fast as she can.

24

Ollis is sitting on a box in the boathouse. She doesn't
know how long she's been there. It's like she's sleeping
with her eyes open. It's as if her entire body and all
her thoughts have been numbed. Or as if she has no
thoughts left. Like they've just trickled out of her head
and disappeared. She has nowhere to go. She's been
rejected. By both her mum and Borgepa. Even by Gro.
But she doesn't feel sad. Or scared. She doesn't feel
anything. Ollis gets up and looks out of the window.
A few clouds have drifted across the clear sky, but it's
still light. Afternoon, soon to be evening. It'll soon get
cold. Ollis picks up her bag, opens it and puts on as
many items of clothing as she can. Layer upon layer
until her bag's almost empty. She closes the flap with
"Borge" written on it. Then she picks up her umbrella.
She leaves the boathouse, walks past the harbour
and down towards the water's edge. She tightens her

grip on the straps of her bag, swings it around once and throws it as far as she can out into the water. It's a good throw. It lands with a splash and then floats, bobbing on the waves. She watches it for a moment before starting to walk.

There's a road along the coast with an embankment sloping down towards the water. The embankment is so steep that you can't see the water's edge from the road, so that's where Ollis walks. If she walks along the road, someone will find her and take her to the police, who are bound to take her back to her mum and Einar. She doesn't want to go back. Ollis heads into town. She's fairly sure it's this way. She's been there before. To buy winter shoes with her mum and to go to the cinema.

Maybe once she gets there she'll be able to make a living selling her inventions. Who knows, maybe the fairy light umbrella will be the next big thing. She could make more mechanical toothbrushes too, or coats with lifejackets sewn into them, or hats with headphones built into them. More clouds gather as Ollis walks and ponders all the smart things she could invent. After a while there's no blue sky in sight. It starts getting darker too, and soon it's almost impossible for Ollis to see where she's going. She lifts the umbrella and opens it, bathing herself and the rocky beach in light.

But Ollis hasn't walked more than a few metres before she's plunged back into darkness. She looks up. All the fairy lights have stopped working. Ollis fiddles with the strings and tries to twist the bulbs, but nothing happens. Frantic, she shakes the umbrella. Oh, no… she can't be left in the dark! The bike lights and headlamps are still working, but they're starting to grow dimmer too. They flicker slightly and then die. It's pitch dark.

Ollis is soon overwhelmed by fear. It starts in her stomach, filtering up into her chest before spreading everywhere else. It's as if the numbness has passed and all her senses have come back to life at the same time, but there's not enough space for them all and it hurts. It feels as if her ribs might splinter into kindling. She throws the umbrella away and drops to her knees on the beach. She pounds her fists against the ground and howls until she's red in the face and her voice cracks, the howl becoming a sob. A tear rolls down her cheek. She touches her face, tracing the path of the tear with her finger. *No*, she thinks. She wipes the moisture away and straightens up. *No. No tears. If I cry now, I'll give up, and I mustn't give up. I'm going into town.* Another droplet of water rolls down Ollis's cheek, but this time it's not a tear. Another hits her forehead. She holds her hands out in front of her and another couple of drops land on her fingers. Ollis gets to her feet. The clouds that have gathered above her are so dark she can barely see the rocky beach, but she starts moving slowly in the same direction she threw the umbrella. It's raining properly now. Ollis tries to walk faster, but the ground is too uneven. Ollis can feel the rain starting to seep through her green hat. It's pouring in rivulets down her forehead. She fumbles her way forward in the dark, and then suddenly there's the umbrella. Ollis moves to take one final step towards it, but doesn't notice that the stone she's standing on is slippery before her foot is sliding out from underneath her. Ollis falls forward, sprawling across the umbrella. She feels it bend under her weight as pain shoots up through her ankle. Ollis whimpers and grabs it in both hands. She can hear her blood roaring. *Don't cry*, she thinks, *just don't cry!* She tries to get up, but when she puts her weight on her injured ankle, the pain is excruciating. The rain

is pouring down now. Ollis picks up the umbrella.
Maybe she can use it as a crutch. But it's completely
bent. She forces it open and lifts it over her head. One
side of it is completely crushed, flapping uselessly.
Ollis straightens up as best she can and staggers slowly
along the beach. She just needs to get into town and
find shelter. But every step she takes is agony. This is
going to take hours. She peers through the dark. She's
pretty sure she can see something in the distance. She
hobbles a bit more quickly. It looks like the outline of
a small house. She limps a bit further. A boathouse!
There's a boathouse fifty metres ahead. Ollis couldn't
have been more relieved if it were a hotel. She hobbles
towards it, along the rocky shore, until a beam of light
suddenly sweeps over her. Ollis stops and looks up
at the umbrella, but it's still dark. She's about to start
moving again when it happens once more, and then a
voice cuts through the rain.

"Olliiiiis?!"

She grinds to a halt. Was that Borgepa?

"Olliiiiis!" she hears again. She peers out from
underneath the umbrella. There's a car up on the road,
and she can see a thin figure with glasses in the beam
of the headlights. Einar. Ollis whirls around and runs
as best she can towards the boathouse. Pain shoots

through her ankle, but Ollis can't worry about that now. She needs to get to the boathouse before Einar catches up with her.

"Stop!" he shouts. Ollis hears stones tumbling down the embankment into the sea. He's coming after her. Ollis tries to move faster. She can see a boat moored to the jetty outside the boathouse. That. She can get away in that. Ollis throws the umbrella aside and speeds up a little. She sees Einar, who has now made it down the embankment, out of the corner of her eye as she reaches the boathouse. Ollis hurries along the jetty towards the boat. There's a set of oars in it. She jumps in and picks up the oars as quickly as she can. She dips them in the water and is about to start rowing when Einar grabs the gunwale with both hands.

"Let go!" Ollis yowls.

"No!" Einar yells through the rain lashing at them. Ollis lifts her right foot and brings it down on his hands as hard as she can. Einar loses his grip. Ollis pulls at the oars with all her strength. She's moving! But Einar jumps to his feet, takes aim and leaps out into the boat. It rocks ominously.

"Get out!" Ollis shrieks.

"No!" Einar hollers. He drops to his knees in front of Ollis and clamps her arms to her sides so she can't row.

"Ollis, what on earth are you doing? We've been looking for you all day!"

"I don't care."

"Your mum is out of her mind with worry!"

Ollis tries her best to twist out of Einar's grip.

"Do you think this is a game?!" His voice is hard. "Someone found your bag in the sea. Ollis, your mum thinks you're dead!"

"How nice for her," Ollis says.

"Nice for her?" Einar asks, his eyes widening behind his thick glasses. "Ollis, stop this now. Let's go home."

"I don't have a home!" Ollis's voice cracks, tears threatening again. She raises her foot to Einar's stomach and tries to kick him away.

"Ollis!"

"No! I saw the wedding invitations!"

"What?"

"Everyone's names were written on them! Yours, Mum's and Ian's. But not mine."

Einar gives Ollis a fearful look.

"What?" he says again. "Oh, Ollis, you've misunderstood. I… I hadn't…" Einar struggles to get the words out. "We wanted you to write your name on them yourself!"

Ollis is suddenly so confused that she stops trying

to get away.

"You're lying!" she shouts, some of the tears spilling down her cheeks, mingling with the rain.

"No, Ollis. I must not have explained very well. Of course we wanted your name on the invitations. After all, you're part of the family. Nothing can change that fact."

"Yes, it can – you!" Her voice trembles and her body shakes. Ollis doesn't know whether it's because of the cold or because she's so angry. Einar lets go of her.

"Ollis, from day one Elisabeth told me you'll always come first. That no matter how much I love her, we could never be together if you weren't okay with it."

"But I'm not okay with it!" Ollis yells. "You took my mum. And Gro doesn't want to be my friend anymore, and Borgepa threw me out. I don't have anyone!" The words tumble out of Ollis, tears streaming down her cheeks. It's as if six months of fog and tears and pain are spilling out of her at the same time. Ollis lets go of the oars and sobs into her arms. She cries all the tears she's held back, and it's as if the pressure in her chest has turned from cement to water, with all the sorrow washing through her. It still hurts, but not in the same way. Then, amidst all her sobs, Ollis suddenly hears one that isn't hers. Einar's face crumples. He takes off his glasses and rubs his eyes. Then he puts his hand on Ollis's head and smoothes it over her sodden hat.

"I'm sorry," he says. "I'm sorry."

They sit there. Ollis and Einar. In a boat by a windswept boathouse. Ollis hides her face and tears in her arms, and Einar lets her cry. He just holds her and runs a comforting hand over her head. Again and again and again. Until the downpour turns to drizzle.

After a while he clears his throat slightly.

"Would you please let me drive you home? Your mum's so worried about you. She's barely functioning – she's just been sitting staring at the phone all day. She won't talk, she won't eat…"

Ollis shakes her head.

"I told her I hated her."

"Ollis, you could tell her you hated her a hundred times more and she'd still love you like crazy."

Ollis looks up and Einar gives her a careful smile. "And as for Gro, she's been cycling around looking for you since sunrise. She's so scared."

"She is?" Ollis asks, amazed. She wipes away some of her tears. "But she's not afraid of anything!"

"Yes, she is," Einar says. "Can we go home now?"

Ollis nods and takes his hand.

25

Einar has dry clothes and a blanket for her in the car. Ollis is so drenched that Einar has to wring out her jacket and trousers. He has food in the car as well. He gives Ollis crackers and a banana. And puts a plaster on the cut on her jaw.

"Did you know you were going to find me?" Ollis asks when she sees how prepared he is.

"I'd hoped I would," Einar says, turning the car around.

Ollis opens the crackers and eats ferociously, crumbs flying everywhere. She hadn't realised how ravenous she was. She's hollow. Like a balloon. The car whizzes along the coastal road, past Hamna and into the village. Past house after house. Ollis peers through windows, watching people switch off lights before bedtime. Entirely unaware of everything that's happened. She's eaten just about all the crackers when her limbs start to get heavy, her head tilts towards the door and she falls into a deep sleep. The kind of sleep that only comes to people who have been out on their own for twenty-four hours.

Ollis doesn't wake up until Einar slows down, indicates and turns onto the gravel track leading up to the house. He stops the car in the yard. Ollis can see something familiar next to the door.

"Is that my pram sled?"

"Oh, is that what you're calling it?" Einar asks. "Billy Kapra dropped it off." He looks over at it as well. "Nice work. Needs new wheels, though."

Ollis gives him a guarded smile.

"Okay," Einar says, looking at Ollis. "I called your mum and told her you're alive. Are you ready to see her?"

Ollis nods and gets out of the car. Everything is like before. The gravel in the yard is the same, the sound of the wind in the trees is the same, Micro and Macro are sound asleep, the house is just the same as she left it yesterday evening, but Ollis still feels like she's been away for years. She heads inside. Like she's done a hundred times before. She kicks off her shoes in the hall. Like she's done a hundred times before. But there's a smell she hasn't smelt for a long time coming from the kitchen. Hot chocolate. Two blue cups emerge into the hall, followed by her mum. She has her red dressing gown on. Her face is a bit pink and her eyes are puffy. She stops in her tracks.

"Hi." Her voice is feeble.

Ollis looks down. She doesn't know what to say. How to explain. But before she can do anything, her mum crumples. Einar only just manages to take the cups of hot chocolate from her before her knees hit the floor and she throws her arms around Ollis's waist. She whimpers and buries her face in her stomach.

"Sorry," Ollis says, tears escaping the corners of her eyes and landing in her mum's bushy hair. Her mum straightens up, shakes her head and smiles.

"I'm so glad you're home."

Ollis doesn't know when she fell asleep. She can't remember going upstairs, laying her head on her pillow or closing her eyes. But when she opens them, the morning sun is trying to force its way past her curtains. Like normal. It's just a normal day. Normal sun behind normal clouds, normal temperature, normal birds singing as they normally do outside her bedroom window. Everything is like normal, and that makes Ollis smile. She gets up. Pulls on her trousers and jumper, shuffles out into the hall and pushes Ian's door open.

"Ah-aah!" he chirps happily from his cot by the window. He's standing with his hands around the bars, drooling and laughing.

"You can stand now?!" Ollis asks. This makes Ian laugh even more.

Ollis lifts him out of his cot and hugs him close. Ian grabs a fistful of her pink hair and crams it into his mouth. She carries him out into the hall and over to the stairs, but then she stops, looking down. She can hear the clink of cups and glasses and a faint humming. She gives Ian a quick smile before heading down the stairs and into the kitchen.

Her mum's face lights up as they come in. She gives them both a hug.

"Good morning, my favourite duo!" she says. Ollis leans into her warm embrace. Then she hands Ian over.

"So Ian's standing up now, huh?"

"… No?" her mum says, looking confused.

"He was when I went in to see him just now."

"He was standing?" her mum asks, astonished.

The kitchen door opens to reveal Einar, his glasses

askew and a look of disbelief on his face.

"He was standing?" he asks.

Ollis's mum skips over to her, grabs her hands and whoops.

"He can stand, he can stand!" she cries, jumping around. But then she stops.

"Oops, everyone hush," she whispers. "We'll wake Gro."

"Gro's here?" Ollis asks, surprised.

"She refused to leave until someone found you," her mum says, stroking Ollis's hair. "But when Einar called to say you were okay she was so exhausted from crying that I put her to bed in the guest room."

"She cried?" Ollis asks. Her mum nods. Ollis looks up at the ceiling.

"Maybe you should go ask her whether she wants some breakfast," Einar suggests.

Ollis nods. She goes upstairs and along the hall. She puts her ear to the guest room door, but she can't hear anything. She opens the door carefully and tiptoes in. Gro is lying on her back with the duvet all the way up to her nose and her short hair sticking up in every direction. Ollis walks over to the bed. She stands listening to Gro breathing in and out, in and out. It's her. In the guest bed. The world's best Gro.

"Sorry," Ollis whispers so quietly it's almost inaudible.

"Look at you, coming in here to say you're sorry while I'm asleep. What a jerk." Gro opens her eyes and looks up at Ollis. "Don't go thinking for a moment you got away with it."

Ollis smiles. Gro sits up.

"I hope you realise I probably cycled ten thousand kilometres looking for you. That's like three Tour de Frances. And when I threw my shoe at Billy Kapra he took me prisoner as punishment. He plied me with fruit squash that was so weak it might as well have been water, and forced me to eat the driest cake known to man, all while I had to listen to him go on and on about why you should never walk across someone else's land."

"Why did you throw your shoe at Billy Kapra?" Ollis asks, wrinkling her nose.

"I had to do something to stop him from catching you!" Gro says, raising her eyebrows.

"It was you that saved me?" Ollis asks.

"Yup." Gro crosses her arms. "But if I'd realised you were running away I'd have let him catch you."

Ollis laughs.

"But what were you doing at Billy Kapra's?!"

"Following you, of course," Gro says. "I saw you hanging your umbrella from our fence out of my bedroom window. Camouflage still isn't your strong suit."

Ollis looks down and starts fiddling with her jumper.

"I…" she says. "I'm sorry I lied about Borgepa. Really."

Gro gives a dismissive wave of her hand. "Better a best friend who lies than one who disappears into thin air and makes me cry for five hours straight."

"But you never cry!"

"I thought you were lying dead in a ditch somewhere! Of course I cried!" Gro says. As if it were the most natural thing in the world. Then she wrings her hands. "Is breakfast ready?"

Gro stays at Ollis's just long enough to demolish three glasses of milk, five slices of bread with salami, a yoghurt and a banana. She also asks for a cup of coffee, but that turns out to be all bravado, because she only manages one sip. Einar watches her, mesmerised. Gro eats just like Ollis did in the car last night. As if she hasn't eaten for a couple of days and is afraid someone might try to take her food away from her. Gro grins at Ollis with banana between her teeth and a milk moustache.

"Yum! Thanks for breakfast!" she says, reaching across the table towards Ollis's mum.

"You're very welcome!" Ollis's mum says, taking her hands and smiling.

Gro does the same with Einar, reaching over and shaking his hand so hard that he slips off his chair.

"Ahoy-hoy!" she says, thumping Ollis on the back before disappearing out of the door.

Ollis looks at her mum and laughs.

Her mum smiles and strokes Ollis's hair. Ollis nods proudly and takes a sip of her juice. She can see her mum and Einar exchanging glances out of the corner of her eye. Her mum clears her throat.

"Ollis?" she asks. "Einar told me what you said in the boat yesterday." Ollis looks at Einar. He fumbles self-consciously with his glasses, his cheeks turning red.

"Yes," he says. "I hope that's okay. I… I…" Einar stammers, fiddling with a crust of bread.

"I'm very pleased you did," her mum interrupts. "But I should have known you weren't happy, Ollis."

Her mum turns to look at Einar again, who jumps to his feet.

"Well… I think we should go for a walk," is all he says before grabbing Ian and heading out of the door.

Now it's just Ollis and her mum.

"Ollis… I've not been paying you enough attention. I've been a bad mother. I… I'm so embarrassed, and I don't know what else I can do except ask for your forgiveness."

Ollis nods in response. Her mum sighs, relieved.

"I realise you felt excluded, but honey, why did you run away?"

Ollis can feel her cheeks getting warm.

"Ollis?"

"I wanted to see Borgepa," Ollis says quietly.

"Borgepa?" her mum asks, tilting her head to the side.

"He's been sending me postcards."

"Has he?" She puts a hand over her mouth. Ollis nods.

"He lives in Hamna. On a boat."

"What?" her mum asks, gaping at Ollis. "He lives in Hamna?! Where we go fishing?" Ollis nods again. Her mum is quiet for a few seconds. "Can I… could I perhaps see the postcards?"

Ollis goes upstairs to her room. She keys in 2-9-0-6 and opens the safe. The pile of postcards fills it from top to bottom. She slides them out and stands there holding them for a moment. Feeling the weight of a hundred and one postcards telling her *I love you*. He's written it a hundred and one times. She closes the safe and takes them downstairs to the kitchen. Her mum takes them from her, careful not to drop any.

"Is it okay if I read them?" Ollis nods. Her mum flicks through the pile. Ollis just sits there and watches all the different places flash by. China, Japan, Australia, Peru, Alaska, Kenya, Italy… Ollis tears her eyes away from the postcards and looks at her mum. Ollis can see tears in her eyes.

"He doesn't mean it," Ollis says quickly. "That he loves me. That's a lie." She tries to smile. To make out like it's a joke. "A hundred and one lies."

Her mum looks up at her.

"Did he say that?" she asks, wiping away a tear. Ollis shrugs.

"Ollis… what I'm about to tell you might be difficult to understand, but I'll try my best to explain." Her mum sits up straight in her chair. "Borge loved… no, Borge *does* love you."

Ollis snorts.

"He does. He loves you so much, but being a father was just too much for him. He couldn't be the dad he wanted to be. It was like he beat himself up inside every day for everything he thought he couldn't do. It was making him ill."

Ollis doesn't say anything.

"Borge's never been good at asking for help. He always wants to fix everything himself. And his way of fixing things was leaving. He thought he was saving you from himself."

Her mum slides the postcards across the table.

"And he asked me never to tell you. He was so scared you'd think he didn't want you."

"But he didn't! And he still doesn't!" Ollis cries. Her mum sighs.

"It was too much for him, Ollis. He was too scared to talk to anyone about it and that fear just got bigger and bigger... He's probably a far better postcard dad. No matter how much he wishes otherwise."

She takes Ollis's hands in hers. They're soft and warm. She leans forward.

"Ollis, it's important to me that you tell me how you're feeling," she says emphatically. "And where you are and what you're thinking... okay?"

"Mm," Ollis mumbles.

"I can't figure it all out myself. That's why you need to be honest with me about what's okay and what you're struggling with. Even if I'm the source of the struggle. I can take it." Her mum smiles. Ollis does too.

"I love you so much. And things can be just as good as they were before. Even with two guys in the house," her mum says, wiggling her eyebrows. For the first time, Ollis knows this to be true. She knows things can be just as good as they were before. She hugs her mum, who hugs her back. Just like before. The wedding needn't be the end of everything. Maybe it'll actually be the beginning of something. Then she remembers. The wedding. The invitations!

"I need to go," Ollis says, jumping to her feet. "But I promise I'll come back," she shouts over her shoulder as she runs out of the kitchen door.

26

"Ahoy-hoy!" Ollis bellows, looking up at the narrow house. No more than three seconds pass before the window flies open.

"Ahoy-hoy!" Gro hollers.

"I need your help!" Ollis says. Gro salutes her.

"Aye, aye!" The window slams shut again, and a moment later Gro's out of the door.

"What's up?"

"We need to go get something from Borgny's."

"Hmm…" Gro says, looking sceptical. "Wouldn't that mean cutting across Billy Kapra's yard?"

Ollis nods.

"Hmm, I did promise him we'd never cross his land again…" Her face cracks into a grin. "But he ought to have realised I had no intention of keeping that promise!"

Ollis laughs as Gro darts past her towards the shed.

Then, suddenly, she grinds to a halt.

"Oh, no! The bikes…"

"What about them?" Ollis asks.

"Dad was so angry when he found out I'd been on Billy Kapra's land that he said I couldn't use the bikes for the rest of the summer."

"That's okay," Ollis says. "I've found a shortcut behind my house, and I've got some ink cartridges we can use to scare the Goat of Christmas Past."

Gro gives Ollis a surprised look.

"Who are you and what have you done with my scaredy-cat of a best friend?"

Ollis laughs and ushers Gro along.

When they get to Ollis's house, Einar is busy with the roses outside the kitchen window. Ollis looks around.

"Where's my pram sled?" she asks. "We need the ink cartridges in the bag hanging from the handlebar."

Einar gets up, brushing soil off his hands.

"It's right here." Einar walks around the side of the house and reappears moments later pushing the pram sled.

"It's working again!" Ollis whoops, rushing forward.

Einar smiles, somewhat embarrassed, and pats the handlebar.

"Yes. I took the liberty of tinkering with it."

"It's great! What did you do?"

Einar crouches down and turns the pram sled on its side.

"If you look here, I've replaced the wheel threads. They were a bit loose. And then here…"

"What's that?" Gro asks, standing a few metres away and staring like she's having an alien encounter.

"My pram sled," Ollis says. "It's part doll's pram, part kicksled."

"Was that what you were riding across the yard that night?"

Gro smacks both hands against her forehead and gawps.

"That's the coolest thing I've ever seen!"

Ollis smiles and turns to look at Einar again.

"Thanks for fixing it."

He blushes and nods. Gro bounds over to the pram sled.

"Look! Look! Look!" she whoops, dancing around it and making Ollis and Einar laugh.

"Can we try it out?" Ollis asks.

"Of course! After all, you built it," Einar says, stepping aside so Ollis can get behind the handlebar. Ollis smiles proudly and pushes the pram sled towards the forest behind the house, Gro lolloping after her.

It's a lot easier to get into the forest now the path is more defined and there're two of them pushing. When they get to the top of the hill, Ollis checks her watch. Quarter past eleven.

"Jump on," she says, nodding towards the kicksled seat.

"You want me to sit?" Gro asks, surprised.

She's in position before Ollis can reply.

"To the birch forest and Borgny the twit!" She looks over her shoulder. "Joking," she snorts.

Ollis kicks off. It handles just as well with two passengers. In fact, it's almost as if it has better purchase, moving forwards like an actual vehicle. They zoom up the track, across the farmyard and into the birch forest.

"Woohoo!" Gro cries, her arms in the air.

With Ollis behind the handlebar and Gro on the seat, the pram sled meanders its way along the winding gravel track. It's the final week of June, and after yesterday's rain the birch forest seems greener than ever. Some rays of sunlight manage to cut through the foliage, tickling Ollis's face. It's good to be back.

They race onwards, soon finding themselves outside Borgny's door. Gro peers disdainfully through the window.

"She's not that bad," Ollis says, patting Gro's shoulder.

Then the door flies open.

"Well, hello there!" Borgny exclaims, grinning down at Ollis. Then she spots Gro. "No!" she yelps, slamming the door closed again. The latch clicks. Ollis sighs and shakes her head at Gro, who looks affronted. Ollis knocks again.

"Borgny?"

"I said no," a muffled voice says from somewhere in the vicinity of the keyhole. Ollis pictures Borgny pressing her mouth up against the other side, just like she pressed her face against the window before.

"Ugh," Gro sighs. Ollis gestures for her to relax.

"She promises to be nice," Ollis tells the door.

"I want to hear her say it," Borgny snuffles.

Gro rolls her eyes, but Ollis raises her eyebrows and waves her closer.

Gro approaches the door somewhat reluctantly, crossing her arms.

"I promise to be nice," Gro says.

"Who's that?"

"It's Gro!" Gro says, waving her arms in exasperation.

"Prove it," Borgny says.

"I can't prove it when you're on the other side of the door!"

Silence for a few seconds.

"Be a pest," Borgny says.

"What?!"

"Be a pest, like you were last time you were here."

Ollis can tell Gro is starting to lose her patience, so she brings her hands together and mouths *please* at her. Gro sighs and turns back to the door.

"Oh, are there any letters for me? Have you got any letters? Could you show me some letters, please…" she squawks in a crude imitation of her past self.

"Aha!" Borgny cries behind the door. "Gro would never have said please."

"Oh, for- it's me, okay?!" Gro yowls.

The door opens. Borgny looks down at Gro.

"And you promise to be nice?"

Gro nods. Borgny takes a step back and lets her in. Ollis smiles at Borgny, who gives her a blank look in return.

"Is it these?" Gro shouts from the kitchen. Ollis and

Borgny go in.

"Is it these what?" Borgny asks.

Ollis walks over to the pile of post Gro is pointing at. She flicks through the envelopes, but it's not them.

"Is it these what?" Borgny asks again.

They keep looking through the pile.

"Oh, you two will always keep secrets from me," Borgny whines.

"I'm looking for some wedding invitations," Ollis tells her.

"Wedding invitations?!" Borgny shrieks. Her eyes are suddenly wild, her hands coming up to tug at her hair. "More like a wedding invasion!"

"Sorry?" Ollis asks, alarmed.

"My letterbox was jammed with them! I had to use a crowbar to get them all out!"

Borgny stomps out of the kitchen, still shrieking. Gro looks at Ollis, eyebrows raised and the corners of her mouth twitching.

"She's not right in the head," she murmurs, but Ollis shushes her. She's never seen Borgny so agitated, and she's on her way back, her heavy footsteps making the cups on the kitchen shelf rattle.

"Fill your boots!" Borgny says, her wild eyes fixed on Ollis. She throws the invitations into the air so that they flutter all over the kitchen. Ollis raises her arms to protect her face. Gro stands rooted to the spot until the final invitation has made its descent, landing squarely in the full cup of coffee sitting on the kitchen table. Then Gro starts laughing. She laughs and laughs, leaning on the kitchen counter. Ollis and Borgny look at each other, and then they start to laugh as well. Ollis has to sit down, and Borgny ends up on the floor, rolling around in the invitations while they howl. Every time the laughter starts to trail off, one of them starts back up again, setting the others off in turn.

After a while, a few bitter cups of coffee and even more laughter later, Gro and Ollis stand at the door with a plastic bag full of wedding invitations.

"Um…" Borgny says. "Feel free to come back sometime. I mean… if you absolutely have to."

Gro and Ollis smile at each other.

"We'd like that," Gro says, bowing.

"Then that's settled," Borgny says.

Ollis and Gro wave goodbye.

"By the way, it's my birthday next Thursday. I'll send you an invite!" Ollis calls.

"Don't bother!" Borgny calls back. "I hate people!"

"I'll send you an invite anyway," Ollis replies,

smiling and waving one last time.

Ollis and Gro fly through the forest. Gro on the kicksled seat with the big postbag in her lap and Ollis behind. They talk and laugh and completely forget that it's way past time for goat walkies. They come shooting out of the birch forest and across the farmyard, right where Billy Kapra is standing.

"Noooo!" Gro yells.

But Ollis leans over the handlebar and gives the pram sled a couple of extra kicks. They're going so fast that Billy Kapra doesn't stand a chance. He bellows at them and shakes his fists. The Goat of Christmas Past sticks his head out from behind the house, but panics when he spots Ollis and the pram sled. He jumps into the air and disappears back around the corner.

"Sorry!" Ollis hollers.

Gro can't even speak she's laughing so hard.

Once they're across the farm and into the forest behind Ollis's house, they're so exhausted from shrieking and laughing that they tip the pram sled sideways and roll into the undergrowth, where they lie gasping for breath.

"Ollis?" Gro says.

"Yes?" Ollis replies.

"Let's never fall out again, okay?"

Ollis turns her head to look at Gro and smiles. "Deal."

That evening, Ollis writes the correct addresses on all the wedding invitations and puts them in the red postbox. Along with a birthday invitation for Borgny. Or 'Brogni', as she's written. That way it will definitely end up in the yellow letterbox. Then, Ollis runs upstairs to her room and digs a pair of old glasses she found in a ditch out of her bedside drawer. She pokes the lenses out before twisting the frame into the shape of a name. She sneaks out into the hall and hangs "Einar" under the ceramic "Elisabeth" sign.

27

It's the twenty-ninth of June. The sun is shining in a clear, blue sky. Ollis is lounging in the prow of the rowing boat, her head over the side and her hands in Lake Nonsvatnet. Refreshingly cold water flows through her fingers with each stroke of the oars. Ollis turns to look at her mum, who is rowing with powerful, regular strokes. Her mum smiles. Ollis smiles too before bringing her hands up out of the water and splashing her in the face.

"Oh, you little…!" her mum laughs. She moves one of the oars down into the water and forwards, forming a wave that drenches Ollis. The water streams from her hair and arms and nose and everything else.

"Mum!" Ollis splutters.

"Happy birthday," her mum says, grinning.

There's a wave of laughter from the shore. Ollis turns and shakes her head resignedly at Einar, Ian and

Gro. They wave.

"Shall we head back?" her mum asks. Ollis nods.

Her mum pulls at the oars, turning the boat and guiding it back towards the shore. Ollis sits up and leans against the prow. There's a warm feeling in her chest.

Back on land, Gro and Einar are laying the picnic table with a lacy white tablecloth, the nice glasses from the living room cabinet and proper plates and spoons. A huge layer cake sits in the middle. Ollis's mouth waters just looking at it. She takes off her shoes, jumps out of the boat and pulls it the last few metres to the shore.

"Time to eat?" she asks.

"Yessiree," Einar says. "Perfect timing. Everything's ready!"

Ollis's mum gets out of the boat and they squeeze around the table. They even have chairs for Micro and Macro. Micro jumps up with ease. He can only just see over the edge of the table. Macro has more trouble. Gro snorts when he falls off his chair for the third time, red fizzy juice streaming out of her mouth and down her white blouse. Ollis's mum decides Macro can sit on the ground.

"Right," she says. "Are we all settled? Please help yourself, Ollis."

As Ollis reaches for the cake slice, there's a rustling from the forest. Ollis stops and everyone turns to look.

"There aren't any bears out here, are there?" Einar asks anxiously. But before anyone can respond, a dishevelled figure with round glasses stumbles into the clearing.

"Hello," Borgny says with a small wave.

She's clearly tried to dress up for the occasion. Her tangle of unruly curls has been piled up on top of her head, secured with what looks like a checked tea towel. And she's wearing a dress. Ollis has never seen Borgny wear a dress before, but on closer inspection she realises it's the crocheted blanket from Borgny's bed. She's cut a somewhat uneven hole in the middle of it, stuck her head through and tied a cord around her waist. The dress is much too long, but she soon trips her way over to Ollis.

"Happy birthday!" she says, shaking her hand.

"Thank you," Ollis says. "I'm so glad you came!"

Borgny nods and turns to look at Macro's abandoned chair. Ollis's mum, who has never seen Borgny before in her life, gets up and moves it back to the table. Then she looks on, bewildered, as Borgny picks it up again and carries it a few metres away from the others before flopping down on it with an exaggerated sigh.

"Interesting choice of venue, I must say."

"This is Borgny," Ollis says, smiling at her mum. "She lives in the birch forest."

Borgny just raises her hand without looking at them. Her eyes are fixed on the cake.

"Are you going to cut that soon?" she asks, pointing.

Everyone helps themselves to the huge cake while Borgny tells them about her most recent letters. Gro and Ollis are riveted. Einar and Ollis's mum try their best to follow the conversation. They don't have a clue what Borgny does or why she receives so much post, but they both smile and nod. Ian just laughs. Drools, laughs and plays with the dogs' ears.

After a while, Ollis's mum claps her hands together.

"Time for presents!"

"Me first!" Gro says, jumping up from her chair. She retrieves a big, soft parcel and puts it in Ollis's lap. "There you go," she says, beaming.

Ollis opens it. It's a camouflage jacket and trousers. Gro smiles slyly. There's also a roll of paper tied with a red ribbon. Ollis opens it. It's two sheets of paper. She reads the first one.

CONTRACT

We can argue, we can laugh,

but let's always be best friends.

Sign here:

The second sheet is the same, but with Gro's name next to 'Sign here'. Ollis borrows a pen from her mum, signs the contract and gives it to Gro.

"Ahoy-hoy," Gro whispers.

"Is it our turn?" Einar asks eagerly. He holds out an envelope and looks expectantly from Ollis's mum to Ollis and then back to her mum again. Her mum laughs and squeezes his hand. Ollis opens the envelope. There are two photographs inside. The first is a picture of a door with a sign on it – 'Ollis's workshop'. She looks at the second photo and jumps to her feet.

"For real?" she whoops. It's a picture of the garage. It's been completely cleared out – and painted! Yellow and turquoise, with boxes labelled 'nails', 'screws', 'spray paint' and so on, all on grey shelves. A large workbench has been set up in the middle of it all.

"Is all this for me?" she asks.

Einar and her mum nod in unison.

"Einar got it all set up," her mum says. Einar blushes.

"Yes. Heh. Well, you know I like tidying up and such… And since you're so good at inventing things… Well, we thought you might like someplace of your own to work on things."

"Thank you!" Ollis says, looking at Einar. "Thank you so much!" Einar nods and blushes even more.

"Er, hello?" Borgny says suddenly from behind a tree. "I have a present for you too, you know."

Ollis laughs and shakes her head apologetically before going over to see Borgny.

"Here," Borgny whispers, pushing something wrapped in crumpled paper and tied with string into Ollis's hands. A wilted buttercup has been tucked under the string. Ollis opens it.

"A letter opener?" she asks.

"Yes. I thought it might be good for you to have your own. You know, so you can come and help with the post whenever you want. You could even bring that one," she says, jerking her head in Gro's direction. "As long as she doesn't moan and whine all the time."

"Thank you!" Ollis says, smiling.

"Yeah, yeah, whatever," Borgny says. "I have something else for you as well." She reaches under her blanket and takes out a postcard. She gives it to Ollis. It has a picture of Hamna on the front. Ollis turns it over.

Hi, Ollis. It's me, it says. *Happy birthday. I love you.*

Ollis runs a hand over the postcard and puts it in her pocket.

"Come on, let's head back," she says. Borgny nods and pats Ollis on the head just a bit too hard before stumbling back over to the table.

Soon everyone has eaten so much cake that they look a bit dazed, their eyes glazed over and their mouths hanging open like zombies.

"Help!" Gro croaks, holding her stomach. Micro and Macro have fallen asleep on the grass, Einar is clearing away the rubbish and plates, and Ollis's mum and Ian have slumped as far down into their camping chair as it's possible to slump. Then Borgny marches past.

"I've got this," she tells Einar, starting to lick cream and cake crumbs from the big platter. Ollis watches them and smiles. With a family like this, having a postcard dad isn't so bad.

Ollis Haalsen lives in a small village in Norway and her full name is **Oda Lise Louise Ingrid Sonja** Haalsen. Her mum picked her long name after five inspirational women who played important roles in Norwegian history. But hardly anyone knows that's her real name. Everyone in her village just calls her Ollis.

O   is for Oda Krohg (1860–1935), an artist/painter. She was also a part of the male dominated political and cultural movement "Kristiania-bohemene" (The bohemians of Kristiania).

L   is for Lise Lindbæk (1905–1961), a writer and journalist and Norway's first female foreign correspondent.

L   is for Louise Isachsen (1875–1932), a doctor and Norway's first female surgeon.

I   is for Ingrid Bjerkås (1901–1980), the first female priest in Norway.

S   is for Sonja Haraldsen, or Queen Sonja of Norway (1937 –), the Queen of course, and for being the wise lady she is, and for her (and Harald's) fight to be allowed to love who you want to love (she was a commoner and the king didn't want her and the crown prince to get married).